Lights! Camera! Cuisine!

Cooking Fabulous Food From the Films You Love

Holly Erickson

Order this book online at www.trafford.com
or email orders@trafford.com

Most Trafford titles are also available at major online book retailers.

Printed in Victoria, BC, Canada.

ISBN: 978-1-4269-0523-0 (sc)
ISBN: 978-1-4269-0524-7 (dj)
ISBN: 978-1-4269-0525-4 (e)

Our mission is to efficiently provide the world's finest, most comprehensive book publishing service, enabling every author to experience success. To find out how to publish your book, your way, and have it available worldwide, visit us online at www.trafford.com

Trafford rev. 5/27/2010

www.trafford.com

North America & international
toll-free: 1 888 232 4444 (USA & Canada)
phone: 250 383 6864 • fax: 812 355 4082

To My Father, Robert Jan Erickson

FOREWORD

Holly Erickson's cookbook appears in the midst of a culture gone food-crazy! These days you can't flip through cable television channels without stumbling into one gripping cook-off or another. From the old days of Julia Child to the Japanese invention "Iron Chef," to the proliferation of reality TV competitions pitting famous chefs against each other in impossible contests, cooking has progressed from a utilitarian skill, to an art form, to "mindless" entertainment. Amidst all this obsessive entertainment, the population is steadily thickening. Bombarded with fast-food advertising, inundated by store shelves bulging with processed food, and so overworked that there's little time to stop and smell the soup (that's not on the stove anyway!), Americans are struggling to reinvent a healthy relationship to food.

Never before have so many people spent so much time thinking about food, writing about it, examining food in all its historic quirkiness, and dissecting food as a profound indicator of culture, geography, and meaning. Countless histories have appeared covering salt, spices, chocolate, coffee, cod, hot dogs, and just about everything else we eat. Michael Pollan has written eloquently about the "omnivore's dilemma" and in "defense of food," anchoring a rising cultural critique of the industrial agriculture system and how it's destroyed taste, cuisine, and ultimately human relationships developed over the sharing of food.

We're haunted by the twin losses of tasty, nourishing, home cooked food and the convivial pleasure of sitting together and enjoying it. We occasionally glimpse this lost paradise in the movies, and it's just those brief encounters that have given rise to this charming cookbook.

How many times have you gone to a movie, found yourself in the dark, alone, watching a mouthwatering feast on celluloid? Perhaps it was a date, and you sat side by side with your enamorada/o, brushing wrists or holding hands, and you felt the tingling thrill of anticipation. The anticipation might be of the love and physical pleasure to come, but might as easily have been the bountiful repast represented before you, that in another time and place you might be sitting down to enjoy yourself.

During such a cinematic moment you might imagine the missing details of the feast on the screen—the resonant odor of a roast, the swirling sounds of sizzling shrimp or the gurgling of a special soup as it simmers on the stove. If you're culinary minded (and you probably are, if you have this volume open before you), you've probably tried to make mental notes of the ingredients, the techniques, and the special flourishes that casually flew across the screen on the way to the Big Meal.

In this quiet contemplation in the cozy darkness of a theater, the social experience that a truly great meal anchors can be overlooked or taken for granted. Of course the characters in the movie are sitting down to dine together, the story is advanced during the gnashing and sipping, funny or sad themes develop, and so on. But it's our own friends and family our thoughts are drifting towards, the pleasure of providing a special meal to loved ones, or even to impress a new love interest.

Finally we have a cookbook that unites the inspiring feasts we've seen in so many movies with our desire to reproduce them in our own lives. Whether your goal is to seduce a special someone as in "Like Water for Chocolate", introduce friends to the full range of French cuisine via "Babette's Feast", or take your party on a tasty trip through the fields and kitchens of southern France via "Jean de Florette", Holly Erickson's tried-and-true menus are here to help you.

I've had the great pleasure of being a guinea pig for several of her Cinematic Feasts, in which we watched the film, pausing periodically for each course, and I can assure you, you will not be disappointed. You'll be inspired to go on exotic shopping trips to find those rare ingredients, but the satisfaction you and yours will have when you sit down together will easily justify it.

Modern cinema can reinforce certain spectatorship and individual isolation, consuming representations of others' experiences as if they were our own. This is both its success and its dark side, perhaps in equal parts. But by taking the representations from their cinematic context and recalibrating them as practical menus for convivial dining, Holly Erickson has turned that hollowness on its head. Instead of watching others feast, we're feasting together. If we're true to the original presentation, perhaps we U.S. eaters, suffering from a food economy dominated by corn syrup and fast food, will reconnect to quality foods, and more importantly, learn to take the time to slow down and enjoy each other as much as the artful presentations and delectable dishes embodied in the menus and recipes herein.

Enjoy!

Chris Carlsson, January 31, 2010

INTRODUCTION

Plain-living Danish sisters sip Champagne and sample caviar drowning in sour cream and butter; drought-stricken Provençal farmers enjoy succulent escargots and plump rabbits; a betrayed wife comforts herself following childbirth with rich, creamy rice pudding---and you're downing stale popcorn and tooth-ruining Jujubes while watching film characters enjoy their gustatory delights. It's not fair! So I wrote this book.

In film, food is a metaphor for practically everything. If a character lacks appetite, it may suggest depression, new love, obsession with a project, or possession of a cerebral bent. A hearty appetite shows zest for life, while an intense appetite can signify greed, vulgarity, or desperation. In "Gone With the Wind", Scarlet O'Hara devours a dirty potato right out of the ground. Her sister-in-law Melanie probably would have waited until it was washed and cooked, then she would have passed it around before taking a ladylike nibble for herself. Chowing down can humble a pompous character or humanize a despicable one, as it does when a sadistic killer becomes just a hungry boy at his mama's kitchen table in "Goodfellas."

When a character tastes an unusual food it can symbolize their awkwardness, or it may show anything from open-mindedness to gullibility. Film characters' table manners might depict social gracelessness, vulgarity, or outright repulsiveness.

How characters prepare food can show expertise, inexperience, ineptitude, quirkiness, ingenuity, or sensuality as when Cate Blanchett rocks out while she's preparing dinner, Sofia Coppola flirts while rolling gnocchi, and Jack Lemmon enlists a tennis racket to drain spaghetti.

Numerous films depict family meals where the food is just awful: the inability to prepare and serve good food shows not just economic hardship, but the poverty of the family relationship. Erotic playfulness is famously depicted in "Tom Jones", "Tampopo", and "Realm of the Senses" to name a few. In "Anna Karenina," Levin's preference for simple Russian fare over the usual French cuisine preferred by his class shows his political beliefs without lengthy diatribes. A most unlikable dinner guest in "Notting Hill" serves up her beliefs by proclaiming simply, "Cooking is murder."

The poisonous apples or mushrooms and child-eating ogres of fairytales become modern films about cannibalism, unsavory sausages, or tainted canolli.

Certain dishes, who cooks them, how they are presented, and who serves them instantly relays historical and social context and relationships.

Food also appears as pure entertainment. The film viewer vicariously experiences anachronistic sumptuousness or shameful gluttony that is fascinating to watch. At a safe distance, film watchers see the cafeteria food fight and the endless pies that have been thrown in faces from Laurel and Hardy to Jack Nicholson.

The addition of food and how humans engage with food is so completely expressive it's a wonder filmmakers need to show anything else to get their points across!

Readers may notice that I have not included many or any recipes from their favorite food-filled film.

In case you hadn't heard, Julia Child has written a few cookbooks of her own, so the abominable "Julie and Julia" is not included.

Fanny Flagg's Original Whistle Stop Cafe Cookbook does the job nicely with plenty of recipes from food served or flung in "Fried Green Tomatoes".

Trying to teach my readers to make the fabulous ramen from "Tampopo" would be like suggesting recreating grandma's incredible chicken soup by dissolving a bouillon cube.

And although I do include one simplified recipe from "Like Water for Chocolate" the novel has many more recipes.

In many films, there are lengthy dining scenes, but what the characters are actually eating is sadly overlooked. We know they order quail in "My Dinner with Andre", but what else for heaven's sake?

So next time you order or rent a film, don't send out for pizza again: thumb through these pages and find something good to eat. Whether you're in the mood for preparing an elaborate array of filmic dishes for an Academy Awards party, or you crave dipping into a hot, gooey fondue while watching "Chocolat", or you just want to sit back and sip a Moulin Rouge while watching Nicole Kidman on a swing---any choice of something to excite your palate will add another dimension to your enjoyment of the films you love.

ACKNOWLEDGEMENTS

Many thanks to:

Alan Zdinak for writing and suggesting film lore and trivia.

R.J. Erickson for financial aid, proofreading and taste testing.

Alexandra Weems for the title.

Mary Anne Weems, Lynn Luthi, and Eddie Ritter for donating and testing recipes.

And to those tireless proofreaders, Scarlett Bartlett, April Hirschman, Margaret Schultz, Janice Wood, and Larry Schorr.

For the cover design, Helen Wilson.

To Chris Carlsson for his foreword.

And the many diners and cooks who helped, prepared dishes, and sometimes even licked their plates at many Film Feast dinners.

THE FILMS

CONTENTS

CHAPTER THREE

CHAPTER FIVE

Dinner Rush (US 2002)

CHAPTER SIX

Tea and Sympathy (US 1956)

Afternoon Teas and Desserts 115

CHAPTER SEVEN

The Children's Hour (UK 1965)

CHAPTER EIGHT

Home for the Holidays (US 1995)

CHAPTER NINE

Covered With Chocolate (Germany 2001)

CHAPTER TEN

Monsoon Wedding (2001)

CHAPTER ONE

Dinner with Friends

Easy to Prepare Meals for an Evening In

The simple phrase "dinner with friends" evokes the pleasure of food shared, of easy conversation and genuine relaxation among people who like each other. Because no friend wants to be exiled in the kitchen, I've made suggestions on how even those challenged by a can opener can contribute simple, transportable dishes to a shared meal. Also, a dinner with friends is the best time to see who can answer the following food-in-film trivia questions.

Dinner With Friends

(US 2001)

Directed by Norman Jewison from a play by Donald Margulies. With Greg Kinnear, Dennis Quaid, Toni Colette, and Andie MacDowell

Dinner With Friends is the realistic portrayal of the rupture of a marriage, and the effect a divorce has on the couple's best friends. Loyalty vs. betrayal, lust vs. lasting love, and friendship itself are all gently examined.

A well-meaning pair of food writers bore their dinner guests with every detail of a recent trip to Italy, including just about every bite of food they tasted on their journey. That's okay. They make up for it by providing the following meal. I've started the menu with a typical Italian champagne cocktail, called Tiziano because it's color mirrors the red hues of Titian's painting.

The Menu

Tiziano
Tomato, Mozzarella, and Basil Salad
Rosemary Roasted Lamb
Summer Squash or Pumpkin Risotto
Almond Polenta Cake
Italian Wine

Tiziano

1 ounce chilled grape juice
4 oz. Prosecco or other sparkling wine

Combine juice and wine in a champagne flute.

Mozzarella, Basil, and Tomato Salad

Buffalo mozzarella or what your grocer has on offer
4 fresh, ripe summer tomatoes
1 bunch fresh basil
Virgin olive oil
Salt and pepper

1. Slice the mozzarella and the tomatoes in ¼ inch slices.
2. Pluck the leaves from the basil stalks.
3. Intersperse the cheese, tomatoes, and the basil on a serving platter.
4. Dribble with good virgin olive oil and sprinkle with course salt and freshly ground pepper.
5. Serve at room temperature.

Rosemary Roasted Lamb

A leg of lamb
Juice of one lemon
Three sprigs of rosemary or more to taste
¼ cup of olive oil

1. Combine the lemon juice, olive oil, and rosemary and spread over the lamb.
2. Make slits in the flesh of the roast with a sharp knife and insert some rosemary sprigs.
3. Cover and marinate in the refrigerator overnight.4.
4. Roast at 300 for 18 minutes per pound or until the inner temperature registers 170 on a meat thermometer, or you can use your outdoor grill according to instructions.

In the film, an autumn dish, pumpkin risotto is included in the menu of this summery meal. I offer you a more estival risotto by suggesting you use summer squash instead of pumpkin.

Summer Squash Risotto

1 large green summer squash or zucchini, diced
1 large yellow summer squash, diced
1 cube butter, 6 T of which to melt with the olive oil
2 T olive oil
1 small onion diced or 2 shallots chopped
7 plus cups chicken or vegetable stock, heated
½ cup white wine
2 ½ cups Arborio rice
½ to 1 cup grated or shaved Parmesan
2 T butter
Fresh ground pepper

1. Melt the butter and oil in a heavy saucepan.

2. Fry the onion and squash in the oil and butter until they are clear and soft.
3. Add the rice and stir to coat it with oil.
4. Add the white wine and stir until it evaporates.
5. Add ½ cup of the heated broth to the rice (it's easiest to use a ladle) and stir until it is absorbed.
6. Continue adding ½ cup stock allowing each addition to be absorbed, while stirring.
7. Just before the rice is tender (about 20 minutes) remove from heat.
8. Add the 2 T of butter and grated Parmesan and pepper.

You needn't be married to the idea of drinking a red wine with this meal just because you are eating lamb. An Italian white is perfectly all right, or a light Italian red will also be fine with the summery side.

Pumpkin Risotto

A two-pound pumpkin, seeded, peeled, and cubed.
Replace the squash with the pumpkin.

Almond Polenta Cake

1 ½ sticks unsalted butter
¾ cup sugar
4 large eggs, separated
1 t grated lemon zest or zest of one lemon
A pinch of salt
1 cup blanched almonds, ground in a food processor
Powdered sugar

Preheat oven to 350.

1. Butter a round nine-inch cake pan.
2. Beat the butter until smooth.
3. Add the sugar and beat until creamy.

4. Beat in the yolks one at a time, mixing fully after each addition.
5. Stir in the zest followed by the ground almonds.
6. Beat the egg whites until fluffy.
7. Fold the whites into the batter one-third at a time adding one third of the cornmeal after each addition of whites.
8. Pour into the cake pan and bake for 30 minutes.
9. Cool and remove from pan.

Powdered sugar may be dusted over the cake surface.
Serve with espresso or strong black coffee.

Mambo Kings

(US 1992)

Directed by Arne Glimcher based on the book by Oscar Hijuelos, with Armande Assante, Antonio Banderas, Cathy Moriarty, and Desi Arnaz Jr. playing a stouter, less handsome, and not as colorful version of his own father, Desi Arnaz Sr.

The slimy, but nonetheless appealing, Assante and the knee bucklingly handsome Banderas are a pair of musical brothers who leave their native Cuba to make their fortune in America. This is a film about music, dancing, family, and love, not a food film. Which is not to say you don't see the family enjoying some of their favorite Cuban dishes. Flan and Ricky Ricardo at the same meal? It's almost too much!

Mambo Kings is an ideal summertime film and menu. Throw a Mambo King dinner on a hot summer evening. Women should wear their brightest, sexiest summer dresses and high heeled sandals; ideally vintage 1950's. Men can wear thin ties and snazzy sharkskin suits or simply floral shirts. Enjoy the movie and the meal and then turn on the CD, roll up the rug and dance! Use the soundtrack album or the Original Mambo Kings, Mambo Mania or any Tito Puente CD.

The Menu

Cuba Libres
Mango Cooler
Avocado in Cumin Lime Vinaigrette
Cuban Three Citrus Pork Roast
Black Beans and Rice
Fried Plantains
Cinnamon Flan
Beer

Cuba Libres

2 oz. Bacardi rum
2 oz. or more Coca Cola
A twist of lime, if desired
Ice

Mango Coolers

1 cup mango pulp
⅔ cup milk
Sugar to taste

Avocado Salad in Cumin Lime Vinaigrette

4 avocados, halved, pitted and peeled
Juice of 2 limes, or more depending on size and juiciness
8 T olive oil
1 t cumin, or more to taste
Salt and pepper to taste

1. Place the avocado halves on their serving dish or dishes face down.
2. Blend the lime, cumin, olive oil, salt, and pepper.
3. Pour over the avocados and garnish with cilantro.

Cuban Three Citrus Pork Roast

4 pounds of boneless pork shoulder, trimmed of fat and tied by butcher
3 T fresh lemon juice
3 T fresh lime juice
½ cup fresh orange juice
½ cup sherry
2 T olive oil
Combine the liquid ingredients.
½ t peppercorns
2 t cumin seeds
4 or more garlic cloves chopped or minced
2 t salt
1 t or more of oregano
1 cup sliced onions

1. Add the spices and the onions to the liquids.
2. Marinate the meat overnight. You can put it all in a plastic kitchen bag turning the bag occasionally as it sits in the refrigerator.
3. Preheat the oven to 325.
4. Place the pork in a roasting pan and cover it with the juices.
5. Roast for about 2 ½ hours.
6. Remove and let rest for fifteen minutes.
7. Carve. Serve with the onions and juices. It can also be served room temperature.

Black Beans and Rice

I've made this dish simple by including canned beans.

2 cans of prepared black beans
2 cups of rice, short grain, prepared
1 green pepper, chopped
4 cloves of garlic, chopped
1 yellow onion, chopped
4 T of olive oil
1 t of cumin or more to taste

Salt and pepper to taste

1. Sauté the onion, pepper, and garlic in the oil.
2. When they are soft, add cumin, the beans and the cooked hot rice and mix.

Fried Plantains

1 plantain or banana per person
Oil for frying

1. Peel and slice the fruit on the diagonal.
2. Heat oil to cover the bottom of a heavy frying pan.
3. Fry bananas until dark brown but not until black.
4. Drain on kitchen paper.

Cinnamon Flan

This can be made the day before.

1½ cup milk
½ cup sweetened condensed milk
½ cup sugar
1 t vanilla
2 eggs, lightly beaten
One cinnamon stick
1 t water
¼ cup sugar
½ t ground cinnamon

1. Add the water and sugar to a saucepan and caramelize over low heat for about five minutes until it turns amber in color.
2. Mix in cinnamon and pour into a 9 X 12 baking dish.
3. Bring the milk to a boil with one stick of cinnamon.
4. Remove the cinnamon.
5. Add the condensed milk and eggs.
6. Blend and pour into the baking dish.

7. Place this dish in a larger dish and pour enough water in the larger dish to go half way up the side of the first dish.
8. Bake for an hour.
9. Remove. And let cool.
10. Chill for at least two hours to overnight in the fridge.
11. Invert onto an attractive serving platter just before serving.

Enchanting Edibles Trivia Quiz

Can you name six films where edibles have magical effects?

1. Peculiar potions and curious cakes make this gal taller or smaller.

2. The offerings of a pastry maker change the attitudes of a straitlaced French town.

3. A Mexican girl uses food to avenge those who have wronged her and to delight those she loves.

4. A Brazilian chef tries to win back her boyfriend through food.

5. A doctored apple causes a young girl to become a live-in caregiver for seven stature challenged men.

6. A wiry old salt finds super strength by ingesting tinned greens.

The Anniversary Party
(US 2001)

Directed by Alan Cumming and Jennifer Jason Leigh, with Alan Cumming, Jennifer Jason Leigh, Gwyneth Paltrow, and Parker Posey.

When Leigh and Cumming, as a troubled Hollywood couple, throw an anniversary party, all their friends are invited. Just to spice things up their loathed next door neighbors and Cumming's ex-girlfriend join the festivities. Leigh gets peevish, an emotion she plays often and well. Ecstasy is imbibed, skinny-dipping ensues, and thus secrets both psychological and physical are revealed. Alter the fashions and change the drugs of choice and this is a party that everyone has been to at some time in their lives.

Almost no guest at this party has an extra ounce on them. So here's a low fat party menu that will keep you trim enough for a clothing optional dip. Although low fat these offerings are full of flavor, color, and texture so you won't suffer any sense of deprivation.

The Menu

Pink Champagne or a Sauvignon Blanc
Goat Cheese Decorated with Flowers
Horseradish Cream Cheese on Celery
Radishes with Goat Cheese and Chives
Grilled Vegetable Skewers
Grilled Chicken and Grape Skewers
Yogurt Curry Dip and Assorted Crudités
Mushroom Pate
Water Crackers

Horseradish Cream Cheese on Celery

One bunch celery
One 8 oz. package of cream cheese
2 T prepared horseradish
Salt and pepper

1. Mix all ingredients.
2. Some of the outer celery may have to be gently peeled if the fiber is tough.
3. Spread the cheese on the stalks.
4. Slice diagonally and plate using celery leaves as garnish.

Radishes with Chive Goat Cheese

One bunch radishes, halved
One 8 oz. package of cream cheese
1 t lemon juice
1 t chives, chopped

1. Blend the cheese, lemon, and chives.
1. Glue the radish halves together with the cheese and chopped chives.

Yogurt Mustard Dip

2 cups plain yogurt, drained
¼ cup chopped fresh dill
2 T Dijon mustard
Salt and pepper to taste

1. Combine the ingredients.
2. Dip any raw or lightly blanched vegetable of choice.

Grilled Chicken and Grape Skewers

1 pound boneless, skinless chicken breasts into one inch chunks
32 large green or red seedless grapes
2 T olive oil
1 T sherry vinegar
4 crushed garlic cloves
1 T lemon juice
Salt and pepper
½ t paprika
A pinch of crushed red pepper
A generous pinch of ground cumin
A pinch nutmeg
A pinch ground cloves

1. Combine all the ingredients.
2. Alternate and skewer the fruit and meat at least 2 hours prior to grilling, or you can marinate in the refrigerator overnight.
3. Grill over a medium hot grill or frying pan for about five minutes or until the chicken just becomes firm to the touch.

Grilled Vegetable Skewers

2 medium zucchini sliced ½ inch thick
2 yellow squash sliced ½ inch thick
2 red bell peppers quartered lengthwise and 2 green and orange or yellow
1 pound cherry tomatoes
½ pound white or brown button mushroom
One eggplant cut into one-inch cubes

Marinade

½ cup olive oil
Salt and pepper
¼ cup fresh basil minced
1 green onion minced

4 cloves garlic minced
2 T fresh ginger minced
2 T lemon juice

1. Blend all the ingredients and marinate the vegetables for at least one hour.
2. Skewer vegetables alternating kinds and leaving about 1/8 of an inch in between.
3. Grill until golden and tender in a medium grill for about fifteen minutes.

Mushroom Pate

Makes two cups

1 T olive oil
1 cup chopped onion
1 clove of garlic minced
½ pound mushroom of any kind
1 T soy sauce
½ t thyme
¼ t nutmeg
A pinch of fresh ground pepper
Salt to taste

1. Sauté the onion and the garlic in the olive oil.
2. Add the mushroom and cook over low heat for about five minutes.
3. Add the other ingredients and simmer for about ten minutes.
4. Puree in a food mill or processor.
5. Transfer to the dish you intend to serve it in and chill.
6. Garnish with parsley and chopped parsley.
7. Serve on crackers or sliced baguette.

Holly Erickson

Heartburn

(US 1986)

Directed by Mike Nichols based on the book by Nora Ephron with Meryl Streep, Jack Nicholson, Stockard Channing, Milos Forman

Nora Ephron is part of a family of screenwriters all of whom enjoy including food in their films, even though as she says, " What my mother believed about cooking is, that if you worked hard and prospered, someone else would do it for you."

In these pages you'll find parents Phoebe and Henry Ephron's film *Desk Set* and sister Amy Ephron's production, *A Little Princess.* Norah Ephron has also written *Cookie* and *Mixed Nuts* and she wrote and directed *Julia and Julie* There are memorable amuse de bouches scenes in *When Harry Met Sally,* ("I'll have what she's having "), *Sleepless in Seattle* (the tiramisu), *You've Got Mail,* and *Hanging Up* (three sisters unleash their tensions in a food fight) all penned by sisters Delia and Nora Ephron.

Inspired by the experiences of Nora Ephron with Watergate journalist Carl Bernstein, *Heartburn* takes us from their meeting to their divorce. Streep portrays a food writer so there are delicious things to eat throughout the film. For Streep's character, feeding people is an act of love. For her husband she prepares pork chops with mustard and cream, lemon chicken, linguini with clams, and pasta carbonara. At frequent dinners with friends (including Czech director Milos Forman, in a cameo) they eat sausage paella, lobster, cole slaw, and key lime pie. Ah the pie, like pies in movies are wont to do, winds up in the face of the philandering Nicholson/Bernstein.

"Rice pudding is a very personal thing," claims Streep's character when friends bring a batch to the hospital following the birth of her second child. As the sheepish Nicholson visits his wife and new baby, her friends feel the need to remind him that his wife loves rice pudding. He replies that he knows. He may be a cheat, but he hasn't forgotten what matters to his wife.

The Menu

Bellini
Pork Chops in Mustard Cream Sauce
Cooked Cole Slaw
Boiled Potatoes
Orange Rice Pudding
Riesling or Gewürztraminer

Bellini

1 ounce peach juice, fresh squeezed or from a bottle
4 oz. champagne or sparkling wine

Pork Chops in Mustard Cream Sauce

8 thin pork chops, boned and trimmed
1 cup cream
2 T Dijon mustard
Salt and pepper
2 T butter or more

1. Melt the butter in a sturdy skillet.
2. Fry the pork chops on either side until brown and firm.
3. Remove the chops and pour the cream into the pan.
4. Add the mustard and blend.
5. When bubbling and blended return the chops to the pans.
6. Cover with sauce and heat through.

Cooked Cole Slaw

One large green cabbage, shredded
Six carrots, shredded
One yellow onion
1 t caraway seeds or more, to taste
A dash of apple cider or favorite vinegar
1 cup or more of water

1. Add the water to a large sauté pan.
2. Toss in the vegetables and steam/fry until cooked but slightly crunchy.
3. Add caraway, salt and pepper, and a dash of vinegar, or omit the vinegar and just add butter.

Serve a Riesling or a Gewurztraminer to accompany this meal.

Orange Rice Pudding

⅓ cup rice
½ cup of water
Pinch of salt
4 cups milk
4 egg yolks
¾ cup sugar or less
Grated rind of one orange
1 t cinnamon
1 t vanilla

1. Parboil the rice in the water with the salt for about five minutes.
2. Drain if there is any leftover water.
3. Bring the milk just to a boil.
4. Add the rice to the milk.

5. Cook for forty-five minutes over low heat stirring now and again.
6. Beat the yolks with the sugar until blended and light in color.
7. Remove the rice from the heat.
8. Add the eggs and rind.
9. Return to fire and stir until thick and creamy, about five minutes.
10. Add vanilla and blend.
11. Sprinkle with cinnamon and garnish with an orange peel or thin orange slices.

Plots That Aren't So Meaty Trivia Quiz

Movies named for meals often set the table for accusations of false advertising. What can the producers expect when their titular repasts are mere walk-ons? For a reward to the winner of this quiz offer a gift certificate to a real meal at a local restaurant.

Identify the following offenders:

1. Not a triple-decker morning sandwich but a Brat Pack feel fest.

2. David Cronenborg whips up a little William Burroughs.

3. Kate and Spencer throw a black and white affair.

4. He came, he ate, and he stayed and stayed, and stayed.

5. The girl once lived on tulip bulbs but now diamonds are her best friends.

How many other films can you name that purport to be about meals? Remember breakfast, lunch, dinner and tea.

Then there are the film titles that promise succulent fruits or savory seasonings. Can you name seven or more fruity film titles? The winner gets a fruit scented candle or soap.

Can you name at least ten film titles that make you salivate when in fact their plots have little to do with the food their names celebrate?

Shhh. Don't tell. The winner receives one of the foods in the movies such as Gingersnaps, Animal Crackers, or Fortune Cookies.

Eat Drink Man Woman

(Taiwan 1994)

Directed by Ang Lee

"Life isn't like cooking at all," bemoans master chef Chu, lonely widower, and the father of three daughters. He has lost not only his sense of taste, but also his zest for life. So paralyzed is his palate, his fellow chef has to sample the food Chu creates. While doing so he compares the tongue-numbed Chu to the deaf composer Beethoven.

"After forty years of Chinese cooking in Taiwan the art is lost. Food from everywhere merges into one, like a river in the sea. Everything tastes the same," complains the depressed Chu, who is also beginning to forget key ingredients in his creations.

Life is no better at home. One daughter works at a fast food joint, another is destined to become an old maid, the third is leaving the family nest to move into an apartment of her own. But that daughter is a fruit that has not fallen far from the tree. Her love of food is evident when she discusses the balance of yin and yang, hot and cold, of colors, flavors, textures, and temperatures.

Life looks up when the widowed mother of a neighbor returns after visiting her daughter in the States. "When I fry rice the smoke alarm goes off! I'd rather die than live there," gripes the mother and sets her hopes to marrying Chef Chu.

The neighbor's little girl buys her lunch at school until Chef Chu steps in and makes her such delicacies as Spare Ribs; Crab with Vegetables, Shrimp and Green Peas, and Bean Sprouts and Sliced Chicken for her lunch pail. That beats packaged mac and cheese any day. The little girl's schoolmates swarm around the aroma of her lovingly prepared lunches.

All the characters have love troubles. One is too prudish, one is too old, one is too young, and one is too self-absorbed it seems ever to find happiness. Love, food, and relationships are interwoven. But in the end, the proof is in the pudding, and men and women eat, drink, and are finally merry.

The scenes of wok cookery, the process of making rice pancakes, even the shots of the kitchen utensils are marvelous. You cannot watch this film without wanting to grab the phone and order Chinese. Some of the dishes are a bit exotic for home cooking if you haven't the equipment needed for Chinese cookery. Joy Luck Dragon Phoenix, Red Seven Star Fish, Jade Prawns, whole shark fin soup, intricately carved honeydew, bitter melon soup and crab dumplings all sound wonderful, but may be hard for a novice to recreate. I've come up with a simpler menu that requires neither Chinese cooking utensils nor the talent of a master Taiwanese chef.

Americans don't often think of Chinese as suitable picnic food, but this menu can be made ahead and enjoyed indoors or out at room temperature. The host should make the seafood salad to keep it refrigerated, but the other dishes can be made in advance and brought over by guests.

The Menu

Chinese Shellfish Salad
Marinated Radishes
Marinated Asparagus
Celery Salad
Broccoli Salad
Curried Noodle Salad
Jasmine Tea
Various Wines

Chinese Shellfish Salad

1 ½ pounds mixed cooked shellfish, shrimp, crab, lobster, scallops, etc
2 cucumbers
2 t finely chopped fresh ginger
2 T soy sauce
2 T vinegar
½ cup peanut oil
2 t sugar
Salt and pepper
Lettuce and or a Chinese cabbage, shredded

1. Cut fish into bite size chunks.
2. Peel cucumbers and cut into matchstick size.
3. Mix ginger, soy, vinegar, oil, sugar, salt and pepper and toss over the fish.
4. Arrange fish on a bed of shredded greens.

Marinated Radishes

2 bunches of radishes
1 t salt
2 T soy sauce
1 T vinegar, rice wine or other light vinegar
1 T brown sugar

2 t sesame oil

1. Wash and whack the radishes with the back of a heavy kitchen knife while leaving them intact.
2. Sprinkle with salt and leave to drain for five minutes.
3. Dress.

Serve chilled or at room temperature.

Marinated Asparagus

2 pounds asparagus, trimmed
4 T soy sauce
2 T brown sugar
2 T olive oil
Pinch salt

1. Simmer asparagus in boiling water for five minutes.
2. Drain, and then run under cold water.
3. Drain again, then dress and serve at room temperature.

Celery Salad

1 bunch celery cut into one-inch lengths
1 t brown sugar
2 t sesame oil
2 t soy sauce

1. Blanch celery quickly in boiling water.
2. Drain, and then run under cold water.
3. Drain again, then dress.
4. Serve at room temperature or chilled.

Broccoli Salad

2 pounds broccoli cut into flowerets

Whisk together:

2 T olive oil
4 t sesame oil
2 t minced garlic
2 T soy sauce
4 T finely chopped scallions

1. Blanch the broccoli.
2. Drain, and then run under cold water.
3. Drain again, then dress.

Serve at room temperature or chilled.

Curried Noodle Salad

12 oz. Chinese egg noodles
2 T peanut oil
2 T soy sauce
1 t curry powder
1 T rice wine or dry sherry
1 t minced fresh ginger
2 t balsamic or rice vinegar
1 T sugar
1 t salt to taste
A pinch of dried red chilies
½ cup minced green onions
½ cup cilantro chopped

1. Whisk together soy sauce; curry, rice wine, ginger, vinegar, sugar, salt, and chill.
2. Cook noodles until just tender.
3. Drain and cool under running cold water.
4. Toss with the dressing and cilantro and scallions.

Gingered Melons

1. Cut ripe Cantaloupe, Crenshaw and or Honeydew melons.
2. Sprinkle with minced candied ginger or place wedges of fresh sliced ginger (sliced to about the size of a small garlic clove) into the flesh of the melon.
3. Chill.

Serve with fortune, rice, or almond cookies or any light wafer.

Serve hot or iced Chinese tea with this meal or a sharp, uncomplicated wine like a dry, white Bordeaux or sauvignon Blanc or Chenin Blanc, Pouilly Fume would go well with the vinegary vegetable dishes, or select a Chardonnay that does not have an oak finish. Rieslings or sparkling wines are another possibility.

For the curried noodles a full-bodied California white, a Gewürztraminer, Riesling, a Sauvignon Blanc, an Oregon Pinot Noir would be lovely, or try a white Graves.

CHAPTER TWO

The Man Who Came to Dinner (US 1939)

Simple Meals for Dining a Deux

"A woman in love burns the soufflés. A woman unhappy in love forgets to turn on the oven," explains the French cooking instructor in Sabrina. In films about love and sex cooking skills and eating habits are evidence of the inner emotional state of a character.

One character may refuse to eat because she has appetite only for her lover. Depressed by romantic rejection another character may pick at his food. A woman demonstrates love by cooking something special for the object of her affection. Young couples endure the discomfort of that first appetite killing family dinner with the relatives to prove their commitment to one another. In real life some sort of eating inevitably accompanies dating and courtship. I've chosen some easy to make, delicious, and sensual movie meals to make for and eat with a lover.

Tom Jones
(US 1962)

Directed by Tony Richardson based on the novel by Henry Fielding with Albert Finney, Susannah York, and Dame Edith Evans.

Tom Jones depicts the bawdy misadventures of an eighteenth century English orphan. This dated, early 60's romp can boast one scene no one ever forgets Tom's seductive, fingers only tavern meal with a lady of indeterminate identity.

Menu

Oysters
Smoked Salmon
Cracked Crab
Boiled Shrimp
Roasted Fowl
Caesar Salad
Ripe Fruits
Syllabub
Wine, Ale, or Cider

The great thing about Tom Jones sensual menu is that even the cooking phobic can recreate this feast. Simply buy cooked and shelled crab and shrimp, some tinned smoked oysters, or some smoked salmon for good measure. Pick up a prepared roasted chicken or prepared chicken wings and drumsticks. If you want to roast your own fowl use the squab recipe from *Jean de Florette,* the roast chicken recipe from *Amarcord*, or game hen from *A Sunday in the Country.*

If you need to have a salad, dress romaine spears with Caesar dressing and eat it with your fingers.

Now all you need is some ripe fruit. If it is winter, buy juicy pears. If you are planning the meal in summertime include juicy nectarines, plums, peaches, cherries or berries. In autumn choose seedless grapes, and green or purple figs. And in late spring serve plenty of strawberries.

Although Tom Jones and his lady friend did not have any dessert you might like to include syllabub. Or add a few gooey chocolate truffles to top off your own seductive feast.

Chill a favorite white wine or try Fuller's London Pride Ale, or for something both dry but fruity, Blackthorne Cider. American ale such as Liberty will also do nicely.

Set your feast on a bare, candle scattered table with neither napkins nor silverware. This is strictly a finger food occasion.

Popular in England from the Elizabethan era until the seventeenth century when Tom Jones takes place; this drink/dessert had a resurgence during the 1960's when the film was made. Although the original dessert did not include ladyfingers, my mother's 1960's version includes them, and so do I as a method of scooping up the creamy pudding.

Syllabub

⅓ cup white wine, cream sherry, Madeira or Port
¼ cup sugar
1 cup whipping cream, whipped stiff
1 lemon, juiced
Packaged ladyfingers from a bakery or grocer

1. Combine the liquor, the lemon juice, and the sugar until dissolved.
2. Blend with the whipped cream.
3. Place in a table pretty bowl and refrigerate.
4. Plate the ladyfingers and serve them alongside the syllabub for scooping.

Cannery Row

(US 1982)

David Ward directed Debra Winger and Nick Nolte in this combination of John Steinbeck's *Cannery Row* and *Sweet Thursday.*

In this less than satisfying film, a marine biologist and a depression era drifter turned prostitute dine together at a pleasant Monterey, California restaurant. Debra Winger, as the heroine, is a lousy prostitute, but quite appealing in the role, so the viewer is happy to see her getting some nourishment, a little luxury, and the promise of a chosen sexual encounter.

Menu

Martinis
Monterey Crab Salad
Tuna in Red Wine Sauce
Rice with Peas
California Red Wine
Cheesecake (See *Satyricon)*

Monterey Crab Salad

2 artichoke bottoms, jarred, frozen, or fresh
½ cup crabmeat, fresh or frozen
French dressing, bottled or make your own
2 hardboiled eggs
Butter lettuce leaves

1. Scoop the crab into the artichoke bottoms.
2. Place on lettuce leaves on salad plates.
3. Slice the egg into quarters and garnish the chokes.
4. Dribble with dressing.

Tuna Steak in Red Wine Sauce

2 T olive oil
2-6 ounce tuna steaks
1 yellow onion, finely chopped
Salt and pepper
½ cup any bold California red wine that you wish to drink with dinner
1 t flour

1. Heat the oil and fry the onion in it until clear.
2. Remove from pan.
3. Sauté the steaks until browned and opaque, about three minutes per side.
4. Remove from pan.
5. Add the flour to the pan and stir.
6. Then add the wine and heat until it thickens.
7. Add the onions and fish to the pan and coat with sauce and serve.

Rice with Peas

One small package frozen peas prepared according to package instructions
2 cups cooked rice, prepared according to package instructions
Butter to taste
Salt and pepper

1. Combine prepared rice and peas.
2. Toss with butter and seasoning and serve.

Serve with the red wine you select for the Tuna in Red Wine Sauce.

Desk Set
(USA 1957)

Walter Lang directed Spencer Tracy and Katharine Hepburn in this Luddite love story of the 1950's. Spencer plays an efficiency expert hired by Hepburn's company. Kate plays a woman about to lose her job to a computer. When the two foes get caught in the rain they wind up dining at her Manhattan apartment. A tough old bird, Spencer fries up some chicken. Lovely but lonely, despite her long-term relationship with a coworker, Kate whips up some floating island. Nothing is more romantic than getting caught in the rain with a potential amour and cozier than watching real life illicit lovers Spencer Tracy and Katharine Hepburn play house.

Menu

Green Salad in Tarragon Vinaigrette
Chicken Breasts With White Wine, Cream & Capers
Wild Rice
Steamed Green Beans
Floating Island

I've dressed up the fried chicken a little for your romantic dinner, but have left the floating island as is for a wonderful end to a dinner à deux. Serve the chicken with white rice, a tossed green salad, and some steamed green beans. Pour the same wine that you use for the chicken

Tarragon Vinaigrette

1 t white wine or cider vinegar
1 t tarragon
Salt and pepper

Blend the above.
6 T olive oil

Add the oil and whisk until emulsified.

Chicken Breasts with Wine, Cream, and Capers

1 T each butter and olive oil
Flour to coat chicken
2 boneless skinless chicken breasts, pounded
½ cup good white wine, serve the remainder with dinner
1 cup heavy cream
2 t capers
Salt and pepper

1. Heat the oil and butter.
2. Coat the chicken in flour, salt, and pepper.
3. Sauté the chicken until it is golden and firm.
4. Remove from heat.
5. Add the wine to the skillet and reduce by half, about 10 minutes.
6. Add the cream and thicken.
7. Add the capers and salt and pepper to taste.
8. Return the chicken to the pan and heat through.
9. Serve with rice.

Floating Island

Islands
3 egg whites beaten until stiff with ¼ cup sugar
2 cups milk, scalded and then simmered gently

1. Poach the islands in the milk until firm, turning over once with a slotted spoon.
2. This will take about four minutes.
3. Don't undercook them or they'll taste eggy.
4. Put them aside on a dish
5. Keep the milk.

Custard Sauce
Milk leftover from poaching
5 egg yolks beaten till pale and dissolved with
½ cup sugar
1 t vanilla

1. Add the warm milk to the egg mixture, stirring.
2. Return to heat.
3. And cook until thick enough to coat the back of a spoon.
4. Stir in the vanilla and allow to cool.

To serve, pour some custard on individual dessert plates and float the islands on a sea of custard.

Serve with jasmine tea.

Jamon, Jamon

(Spain 1992)

Jose Juan Bigas Luna directed Penelope Cruz in this romantic farce about class and food. Penelope Cruz' character creates an exceptional tortilla Espagnol. That's all I have to say about this movie. I include it because I love tapas. My second cooking job after culinary school was at the first tapas/antipasti bar in San Francisco. I loved their grub.

To create a simple Spanish picnic for you and a loved one, simply make the tortilla (which is eaten at room temperature) and purchase the rest. Ice a bottle of Spanish wine, or cava, and you're set.

Menu

Marcona Almonds
Manchego Cheese
Serrano Ham
Spanish Olives
Tortilla Espagnol

Holly Erickson

Tortilla Espagnol

½ cup olive oil
2 garlic cloves
1 ½ pound of potatoes, peeled, quartered lengthwise, and sliced in 1/8 inch slices
1 medium yellow onion, finely sliced
Salt to taste
Cayenne to taste
6 eggs, well beaten
Store bought or homemade salsa, as desired

1. Heat the oil in a nine-inch skillet.
2. Add the garlic and sauté until golden.
3. Remove and discard the garlic.
4. Add potatoes and onion, and salt.
5. Cook over low heat until the potatoes are tender, but not brown, about 15 minutes.
6. Remove from skillet pat them dry with a kitchen towel.
7. Add the eggs to the potatoes and coat well.
8. Add more oil to the skillet and bring to high heat.
9. Add the potato mixture and pat down so the spuds are covered by egg.
10. Reduce flame to low heat and cook until browned.
11. Place a plate over the skillet.
12. Turn the pan onto the plate.
13. Return the tortilla to the skillet on the uncooked side and continue cooking until browned.
14. Flip onto plate. The inside is traditionally a little runny.
15. Slice into wedges.
16. Serve hot or cold with salsa on the side.

Serve hot or cold sliced into wedges.

La Grand Bouffe

(France 1973)

Marco Ferreri directed Michel Piccoli and Philippe Noiret. Four friends rent a villa and eat themselves to death in this famous, but unappetizing film. The food depicted in the movie ranges from the very simple such as bouillon and baguettes, to an array of foul; duck, pullet, and goose, braised in sherry, port, and champagne respectively. The gluttons even eat pizza and down hot water laced with sugar to aid their digestion.

For La Grand Bouffe almost any good eating will do. For fun, indulge your lover to a weird array of his or her favorite dishes that you would not ordinarily eat at the same sitting. Some wedding clients for my catering company once created a menu of all the dishes they enjoyed while courting. BLTs, chicken caesars, caramel sundaes, mac and cheese. For a wedding? Why not? Who is to say what is the food of love. You decide.

Can you name several scenes of unparalleled gluttony?

Sabrina

(US 1954)

Billy Wilder directed Humphrey Bogart and Audrey Hepburn in this classic. Always adorable, Audrey spends too much time moping over a cad. His brother, played by Bogey seems like an old fogey next to the luminous Hepburn. But the fashion is fantastic and the cooking school scenes are great fun. Once Audrey learns how to cook she also learns how to really love, rather than adore from afar. The remake of the film starring, Julia Ormand, takes place at fashion school, rather than cooking school, hence it loses all its charm.

"We must be merciful when we crack an egg…" explains the pre-vegan French chef who instructs young Sabrina in a Paris cooking school. "The soufflé must be high like two butterflies dancing in the summer breeze."

I will teach you to make a frothy fail proof soufflé and yummy mousse to serve as a light meal for two. You can make the mousse ahead so you can pay more attention to your amour.

Menu

Green Salad with Mustard Vinaigrette
Dancing Butterfly Cheese Soufflé
French Bread and Sweet Butter
Sabrina's Chocolate Mousse
A French white wine
Strong Coffee

Mustard Vinaigrette

1 t champagne vinegar
1 t Dijon mustard
Salt and pepper

Blend the above.

6 T olive oil

Add the oil and whisk until emulsified.

Dancing Butterfly Cheese Soufflé

2 T butter, plus some for greasing the dish
2 t flour
½ cup milk
½ cup Gruyere, Cheddar, pepper jack or goat cheese
2 room temperature eggs, separated (You can warm cold eggs by placing them in tepid water)
A pinch of salt
A pinch of nutmeg
A pinch of cayenne

1. Preheat the oven to 375; do not open the oven door until you put in the soufflé.
2. Butter two 8 oz. ramekins, one 16 oz. soufflé dish or a deep casserole.
3. Melt the butter in a saucepan.
4. Stir in the flour.
5. Cook for sixty seconds.
6. Whisk in the milk.
7. Bring to a simmer, stirring all the while, and do not let boil.
8. Remove from the flame.
9. Stir in the cheese.
10. Add part of the cheese mixture to the yolks.
11. Then add that to the rest of the cheese mixture and blend.
12. Beat the whites in a clean bowl with a clean whisk. No residual oil or fat should be on the whisks or bowl or the whites won't rise.
13. Beat until the peaks are stiff, but not dry, do not over or under beat. Under beaten whites will not hold a peak, overbeaten they begin to separate. If you overbeat you can add an extra egg white and re-whisk.
14. Stir a scoop of the whites gently into the cheese mixture.
15. Then gingerly add the remaining whites.
16. Gently pour into the ramekins.
17. You don't want to lose the air bubbles that have formed in the egg whites.
18. Bake until puffy, golden about 20 minutes or 40 minutes for the larger dish.
19. If you use a dish other than a straight-sided ramekin or soufflé dish the soufflé will taste as good but won't rise as high.
20. The center should look runny

Serve at once with a tossed green salad with mustard vinaigrette.

The soufflé will begin to fall shortly after it is out of the oven. This is the way of soufflé, not a failure on your part.

Sabrina's Chocolate Mousse

7 oz. bittersweet chocolate
4 T hot water
4 T sugar
6 T water
3 cups whipping cream
1 t vanilla
1 ½ cups sugar
Fresh mint springs for garnish

1. Melt the chocolate and 4 T water gently over heat in a bain-Marie or double boiler.
2. Add the 4 T sugar and the 6 T of water.
3. Bring to a boil then take off heat and allow to cool.
4. Whip the cream to a firm consistency.
5. Add vanilla and the remaining sugar.
6. Blend the whipped cream and chocolate.
7. Spoon into pretty individual serving bowls or one attractive serving bowl and chill until ready to serve.

Serve with fresh mint garnish and additional whipped cream.

CHAPTER THREE

A Family Affair (US 1937)

Hearty Yet Simple Family Fare

Dining among relatives is among the most familiar of human experiences. Meals can be eagerly anticipated for the satisfaction of both physical and psychic nourishment and for the companionship and gustatory pleasure they afford. Or they can be dreaded as a source of tension, resentment, and indigestion.

Cinematic family meals are a showcase for family traditions and habits and just as often for neurosis and prejudice. Some Americans, dismayed by fast food culture, idealize the dining rituals of other cultures. But the Taiwanese daughter from Eat Drink Man Woman refers to the exquisite weekly meals prepared by her chef father as the "Sunday Dinner Torture Ritual." That would be a good term for many of the family meals depicted in movies.

One of the most agonizing family dinner scenes ever filmed is in Dogma #1 or The Celebration. At the patriarch's birthday celebration, dozens of family members, employees, and friends are treated to venison and lobster along with the unappetizing revelation that the man of honor has raped two of his children. Bon appétit.

But there are also many funny and appetizing family meals depicted in film. I've chosen several international films where humor tenderizes tension and warm family feeling seasons ordinary meals. Phew!

Amarcord

(Italy 1974)

Directed by Federico Fellini with Bruno Zanin, Pupella Maggio, and Armando Brancia.

This masterpiece is both a fond reminiscence of life in prewar Italy and a rueful look at male adolescence. Following the life of a town over one year, it's bursting with characters, laced with magical incidents, and spiced with scatological pranks. Its spirit is so buoyant that even death and the specter of Fascism can't drag this movie down. The irrepressible Nino Rota score doesn't hurt either.

A family dinner pictured in Amarcord is simple, yet bountiful enough for a dinner party. And the dishes are easy enough so that perhaps your children can help prepare this meal with you.

Menu

Crispy Italian bread
Pastini in Brodo
Roman Spaghetti with Pecorino
Roast Chicken with Sage and Marsala
Peas with Prosciutto
Salad with Italian Dressing
Italian Pastries
San Genovese wine

If you're serving this meal for friends play Nina Rota's Omaggio-A Homage to Federico Fellini to create the mood and evoke memories of all of Fellini's work.

Broth with pasta is a great way to start a meal. Kids love it since it's a version of that universal juvenile favorite, chicken noodle soup. Adults would also do well to start with a light broth so as not to eat quite so much of the following courses.

Pastini in Brodo

Homemade or store bought chicken broth

Di Cecco or other brand pastini

1. Cook the pasta according to package directions while heating the broth.
2. Add the drained pastini to the broth.
3. Season with salt and pepper.
4. Serve with grated Parmesan.

Roman Spaghetti with Pecorino

Spaghetti
Pecorino Romano cheese
Fresh ground black pepper

1. Cook the pasta according to the instructions on the package.
2. Drain but do not rinse the pasta.
3. Sprinkle with pecorino and season with black pepper.

Roast Chicken With Sage and Marsala

One roasting chicken
One bunch of fresh sage
2 T butter
Salt and pepper
½ cup of Marsala wine

1. Preheat the oven to 425.
2. Dry the chicken inside and out with paper towel.
3. Stuff the cavity of the chicken with the sage.
4. Rub butter on the outside of the chicken and sprinkle with salt and pepper.
5. Roast for fifteen minutes.
6. Reduce the heat to 350 and roast for an additional hour for a small bird or an hour and fifteen minutes for a larger bird.

7. Pour half the Marsala over the chicken once the skin is brown and baste every so often while the bird is roasting.
8. Allow the roasted bird to sit for ten to fifteen minutes before serving.
9. Serve the chicken with the drippings as a sauce, adding a dash of Marsala for the adults.

Peas With Prosciutto

One ounce of Prosciutto, chopped with visible fat removed
One small yellow onion, chopped
One package frozen peas
Olive oil to cover a sauté pan
Pepper

1. Sauté the onion until lightly browned.
2. Cook the peas according to the package.
3. Combine with Prosciutto.
4. Add fresh ground pepper for seasoning. Because the ham is salty use additional salt with discretion

Salad with Italian Dressing

Bottled Italian dressing or olive oil, red wine vinegar, salt, and pepper served at table so diners can dress their own lettuce

Complete this meal with a selection of Italian pastries from your local bakery. Canolli or almond tarts are just two suggestions. If there is no handy Italian bakery, many grocery stores carry a line of Italian sweets. Stella D'Oro, De Musso, Biancoforno, Lazzaroni, and Fornobohome are just a few of the brands available. You can purchase chocolate florentines, cantucci, amoretti, lemon cookies, or other Italian favorites. For something more extravagant, you can order some delicious pastries from Dean and De Luca or Riulli, online. Or make the canolli or other Italian pastries from other movie recipes that are listed in the recipe index. Serve with espresso or strong coffee and you have completed a typical old-fashioned Italian family meal. Of course, today Italian families eat internationally influenced food like everyone else.

Gross Grub and Vile Viands Trivia Quiz

Can you think of ten films where really disgusting food is eaten? Reward the winner with a jar of gummi worms.

1. Free-spirit Jane Fonda sets up her widowed suburban mother with an eccentric French gentleman, who on their first date serves fried eel and green olive balls.

2. Debra Winger's character recalls an old beau ordering a beer milkshake, which inspires Nick Nolte's character to do the same. There's a reason this frozen novelty hasn't caught on. But try one anyway!

3. American viewers may pale at the thought of French fries in a curry sauce, but it's popular fast food dish in the UK.

4. Have you ever craved pissing shrimp or pissing beef balls? Not yet? You may after seeing this film. They squirt their juices just like Chicken Kiev.

5. Minnie Driver, a Victorian era Jewess passing as Christian for economic reasons, eats semolina pudding for the first time at the home where she is employed as a governess. She and her sister had discussed in their girlhoods what semolina might resemble... which two giggling virgins could only imagine...

6. Got no milk? Try Cola on your Lucky Charms.

7. Have another helping of clamshell soup.

8. "Your produce was worth the trip," claims an alien while munching a banana with the skin still on.

9. Real men don't eat Prune Quiche. Nor Ham and Clam, Liver and Lager, nor Pork Ciste The well-bred daughter of an English lord spits her first bite of a ghastly dinner onto her plate.

10. A solution to bad manners and vile food follows when the Spanish Civil War refugee living with the family offers to spice up the fare.

11. Even though it's a cruel gruel he still wants more.

12. Mel Gibson noshes out of a dog food can.

13. Sly slurps down a blenderful of raw eggs.

14. A devil-may-care attitude prompts Mia Farrow to indulge herself with a snack of raw liver.

15. After plants and animals have become extinct, the government feeds people with an algae-green liquid.

16. A private dining club serves its members endangered species.

17. Greasy roach-mobile fish and chips are served out of this vehicle in a film of the same name.

18. A belle époque French actrice claims that enjoying this delicacy is like kissing snow. What are the film and the delicacy?

19. Cate Blanchett rocks and rolls out a gourmet feast for her indifferent husband.

20. Buddy likes maple syrup with his pasta.

Catfish in Black Bean Sauce

(US 2000)

Directed by Chi Moui Lo with Sanaa Lathar, Paul Winfield, Mary Alice, and Lauren Tom.

"That stuff could clean silverware!" complains Mary Alice about the sauce her daughter's birth mother has brought from Viet Nam.

In this little known but charming film, a kindly African American couple adopts two Vietnamese war orphans. Once they are grown, the children discover that their mother is still living. The children represent the extremes of adopted children. The daughter has idealized her mother and wishes nothing in life more than to meet her. The son is indifferent to meeting his birth mother and worries that it would hurt his Mom's feelings. The disappointments, misunderstandings, and cultural differences that result when the frankly unlikable mother arrives from Viet Nam are the gist of this sweet and funny movie. The title of the movie combines a favorite southern African American dish, catfish, with black bean sauce, a ubiquitous Asian favorite.

Menu

Catfish with Black Bean Sauce
Stir Fried Bok Choy or Collard Greens
Steamed Rice
Vietnamese Ice Coffee or Tea

Catfish in Black Bean Sauce

Adapted from a recipe by Jeremiah Tower, my teacher at cooking school and Mark Franz, a fellow student there.

1 catfish per person
A great deal of peanut oil, heated
½ cup cornstarch
2 cups fish stock
1 t salt

2 oz. finely chopped ginger
½ cup black bean sauce, prepared (see below for recipe or buy)
2 T butter
2 T sesame oil
2 chopped green chives

1. Combine the salt and cornstarch on a plate.
2. Roll the fish in it, and then shake off any excess.
3. Put the stock and ginger in a saucepan.
4. Boil over high heat for three minutes.
5. Fry the fish in the hot oil for about eight minutes, being careful not to overcook.
6. Add the black beans to the stock.
7. Add butter and sesame oil.
8. Place the fish on paper towels to absorb any excess oil.
9. Plate or platter the fish on prepared rice or rice noodles.
10. Pour the sauce over the fish and garnish with chives.

Black Bean Sauce

2 t fermented black beans
2 t minced garlic
½ t sugar
¾ t sesame oil
¾ t rice wine
½ t salt
4 thin slices fresh ginger
1 green onion sliced diagonally
Soy sauce
Peanut oil

1. Rinse the beans.
2. Mash with garlic and sugar.
3. Add oil, rice wine, pepper.
4. Add the rest of the ingredients and warm through.

A Sunday in the Country

(France 1984)

Directed by Bertrand Tavernier with Louise Ducreux, Sabine Azema, and Michel Aumont.

A gentle film lazy as a warm Sunday afternoon explores the vicissitudes of fatherly love. A glamorous, thoroughly modern (circa 1910) Parisienne visits her doting father, a painter, at his comfortable country house. A kind but stuffy brother and his dull family sharpen the impressionistic idyll.

The family, luckily for our purposes, eats all day long. They enjoy dinner, afternoon tea, a jaunt to a café, and supper. "A little excess never hurt anyone," proclaims the patriarch. It's enough to make the modern person quake with anxiety about weight gain. But my menu combines the best dishes of their meals into one.

Play some dreamy Debussy, Ravel, or Erik Satie for this meal.

Menu

Crusty Bread and Butter
Pate
Lemon Roasted Game Hens
Potatoes Gratin
Carrots à la Parisienne
Salad with Mustard Vinaigrette
Palmiers
Coffee
Benedictine

—

"Baking can be learned, but roasting is an art you are born with," claims the father.

Lemon Roasted Game Hens

½ cup softened butter
1 t lemon zest
Salt
Pepper
⅔ cup dry French white wine that you'll be drinking with dinner

1. Preheat the oven to 425.
2. Rinse and pat dry the birds inside and outside with paper towel.
3. Mash together the butter with salt and pepper and lemon zest.
4. Place half the butter under the skin.
5. Rub the birds externally with the remaining butter.
6. Roast for 45 minutes to 1½ hours according to the instructions on the wrappings of the hens.
7. Pour the wine over the birds and pour off the drippings and serve over the hens.

Potatoes Gratin

2 T butter
½ cup sliced shallots
1 crushed garlic clove
2 peeled, thinly sliced russets
1 ½ cups heavy cream
1 cup shredded Gruyere cheese
Salt and pepper

1. Butter the baking dish.
2. Spread the shallots around.
3. Fan the potatoes over the shallots.
4. Scatter with cheese.
5. Pour the cream to submerge the potatoes.
6. Sprinkle salt and pepper to taste.
7. Bake for 1½ hours at 375.

Carrots à la Parisienne

3 cups sliced carrots
1 T butter
1 T sugar
Juice of ½ lemon
Chervil, dill, tarragon or thyme any herb that you have on hand that pleases you.
Salt and pepper

1. Slice the carrots diagonally.
2. Parboil for ten minutes.
3. In a sauté pan add lemon juice, butter, sugar, salt and cook down until shiny.
4. Add the carrots and cook over low heat until tender until tender over low heat.
5. Add herbs.

Palmiers

1 pound thawed puff pastry
Sugar

1. Preheat oven to 425.
2. Roll the dough into strips 6 inches wide by 20 inches long.
3. Brush dough with water.
4. Fold the sides to meet in the middle.
5. Sprinkle with sugar.
6. Fold lengthwise in half to form a four-layer strip.
7. Chill covered for 20 minutes.
8. Cut crossways into ½ inch strips.
9. Place on a lightly buttered baking sheet.
10. Form an inverted "V" with the cookies.
11. Bake until caramelized, about ten minutes.
12. Turn over sprinkle with sugar again and bake another 5 minutes.

Quality Time It's Not Trivia Quiz

Numerous films depict family meals where the food is just awful and the resentment so thick you could carve it like a turkey. Name the following funny or emotionally wrenching family dinner scenes. The prize should be a copy of *Miss Manners Guide to Domestic Tranquility*.

1. Pass the asparagus, please!

2. A New York Jew feels as if he is auditioning to be the boyfriend of a WASP Diane Keaton.

3. A jittery family serves a spaghetti dinner to a trio of unusual bank robbers.

4. A guy brings his girl over for a family dinner to impress his parents, but in reality she's a stranger he has kidnapped for the evening.

5. "This sauce could clean silverware."

6. "Dad used to take the two of us into the library and rape us." a Danish man announces while making a toast at his father's birthday dinner.

7. "You don't eat much, you don't talk much." says a grandmotherly woman to her green-faced houseguest not knowing he has just witnessed a gruesome murder.

8. The holiday bird does a lap dance.

9. Will you tell the story about the clamshell soup again?

10. Do we have to?

11. Guess who's coming to dinner? At a London barbecue.

12. So you want to know the meaning of Thanksgiving? Let Christina Ricci tell you.

13. "You cut da toikey?" A close-knit family unravels when suburban living distances cause part of the family to be late for Thanksgiving.

14. The Santa Lucia Christmas tradition is bastardized, and then interrupted, when a burglar comes to dinner.

15. We want meat! The children at a Swedish vegetarian commune revolt.

16. An engaged couple has their first dinner with both sets of parents; one is a senator and three are men.

17. A slaphappy Brooklyn family goes at it over dinner while the son is dying to disco.

18. A son-in-law to be rambles an impromptu grace before a first family meal.

19. An amateur parent decorates the kitchen with rice pilaf and gives the gift of food poisoning.

Moonstruck

(US 1987)

Norman Jewison directed Cher, Olympia Dukakis, and Nicholas Cage in the beloved film that extols tradition and family and passion and spontaneity and eccentricity all at the same time. Olympia DuKakis as the matriarch is marvelous and what she cooks and eats tell much about her character. "Don't shit where you eat," she proclaims, as a warning to her errant husband. The family eats all American-Italian favorites such as manicotti and canolli. And Cher cooks a rare steak for her new hotheaded lover saying it will "feed your blood". Olympia Dukakis, when she suspects her husband may be cheating, goes by herself to the family's favorite neighborhood restaurant. She orders traditional fare, nothing trendy, for this is what will sustain her and her family. And while enjoying her meal, she regains her equilibrium and maintains her dignity. Her self-possession even attracts the silver haired college professor at a neighboring table.

Menu

Rare Roman Ribeye
Moonstruck Manicotti
Broccolini Sautéed with Garlic
Salad
Bought Canolli
Red Italian wine
Espresso

Rare Roman Ribeye

Rib Eye Steak
Salt and Pepper
Lemon

Simply broil a steak to you liking and serve with lemon wedges.

Broccolini Sautéed with Garlic

Broccolini
Olive oil
Garlic, sliced

1. Cut the thick ends off of the broccolini.
2. Heat a sauté pan and add the olive oil and garlic.
3. When the garlic is golden, remove it.
4. Add the broccolini and sauté until tender.

Manicotti

1 cup flour
1 cup water
A pinch of salt
7 eggs

2 pounds ricotta cheese
2 t chopped fresh basil or 1 t dried
A pinch of hot pepper flakes
¾ cup grated Parmesan or Romano
A healthy pinch of pepper
½ pound mozzarella

1 large can tomato sauce or a large jar of your favorite pasta sauce

Makes 12-14 pancakes.

1. Combine the flour salt, and water.
2. Beat until smooth.
3. Add 4 of the eggs beating after each addition.
4. Heat a crepe pan or small 5 to 6 inch skillet with a few drops of olive oil.
5. Place about 3 T of batter into the hot pan, using a small ladle.
6. Distribute.

7. Cook over low heat until firm but not browned.
8. Turn over with a fork or spatula.
9. Cook on other side.
10. Use all the batter. There is no need to add oil to skillet each time. Reserve the cooked crepes. You'll be reheating them so there is no need to keep them warm.
11. Combine the salt, 3 eggs, ricotta, basil, pepper flakes, and half the Parmesan.
12. Place 2 T filling and 1 strip of mozzarella on each crepe, then roll.
13. Place seam side down in a large buttered baking dish.
14. Cover with tomato sauce and the remaining cheese.
15. Bake at 350 for 45 minutes.

Soul Food

(US 1997)

George Tillman Jr. directed Vanessa Williams, Viveca Fox, and Nia Long in the movie that evolved into a popular television series. This supposedly heartwarming film has no one to like in it but the young narrator. He tries to keep the family; nastily rivalrous sisters, a mentally ill uncle, a cheating husband, a recidivist con, an ice queen lawyer, a lecherous pastor, and the beloved grandma who slowly committed suicide by not taking her medicine. But there is plenty of good food to see.

"Bless this bread,
Bless this meat,
And bless this stomach,
Cuz I's gonna eat!"

is the blessing muttered over dinners, which might include:

Deep-fried Catfish
Mac and Cheese
Chicken and Biscuits

Ham with Canned Pineapple
Cornbread
Chitlins
Greens
String beans
Black-eyed Peas
Cobbler
Egg Pie
Sweet Ice Tea

With Big Mama's diabetes?
I've simplified and lightened up this feast. But not that lite!

Menu

Catfish Stew
Collards and Rice
Cornbread
Mac and Cheese
Apple and Peach Cobbler

Catfish Stew

1 pound catfish fillets, cut into two inch strips
One can tomatoes
1 onion, chopped
2 cloves garlic
1 cup clam juice
Salt and pepper
Tabasco

1. Add everything but the fish to a pot.
2. Bring to a boil, and then cook for ten minutes at medium heat.
3. Add fish and simmer for five minutes or until the fish is flakey.
4. Serve over collards and rice.
5. Add a dash of Tabasco sauce if desired.

This uses the recipe from "Johnson Family Dinner"

Collards and Rice

3 cups chopped collard greens
1 cup rice
2 cups vegetable broth
1 T butter
Salt

1. Boil the stock.
2. Reduce heat.
3. Add the rice and veg and simmer for 20 minutes until the rice is tender and the liquid is absorbed.

Cornbread

1 cup sour milk or buttermilk
1 scant t baking soda

Combine:
1 T butter
¾ cup sugar
Cream with
1 beaten egg

Sift:
1 cup yellow cornmeal
1 cup flour
1 t baking powder

1. Preheat oven to 350.
2. Blend all ingredients.
3. If the mixture is a little too thin, add more cornmeal.
4. Pour into a greased 8x8 or 9x9 inch baking pan and bake until golden brown. Check at 20 minutes and often it will take longer.
5. Serve hot and dripping in butter.

Mac and Cheese

1 cup macaroni, cooked according to instructions
1 cup grated cheddar, mild or sharp or both
½ cup Muenster cheese
⅔ cup milk
¼ cup breadcrumbs
1 large egg
Salt
Paprika

1. Layer most of the cheese and macaroni in a buttered baking dish.
2. Beat the egg and add to the milk and salt.
3. Pour over the mac and cheese.
4. Sprinkle with any leftover cheese, and the breadcrumbs and paprika.
5. Bake at 400 until browned.

Peach and Apple Cobbler

½ cup sugar
1 T cornstarch
½ t cinnamon
2 cups sliced peaches
1 cup sliced, peeled green apples
Juice of ½ lemon
3 T lard
1 cup flour
1 T sugar
1 ½ t baking powder
½ t salt
½ cup milk

1. Heat the oven to 400.
2. Mix ½ cup sugar, the cornstarch and cinnamon in a saucepan.

3. Stir in the fruits and the lemon juice.
4. Cook until mixture boils and thickens, stirring every so often.
5. Boil one minute.
6. Pour into an ungreased baking dish.
7. Mix the dry ingredients and cut the shortening in until the mixture resembles uncooked oatmeal.
8. Stir in milk.
9. Drop by spoonfuls onto the fruit mixture.
10. Bake until golden about 25 or 30 minutes.

Food on Television Trivia Quiz

1. Charleston era wannabe aristos out dine each other.

2. A neurotic British chef whips up comedy.

3. A cockney urchin becomes a chef, an hotelier, and a lover of the gourmand Prince of Wales.

4. Zees Belgian he has ze perfect palette.

5. It's a family show; is that blood or marinara sauce

6. Murder and cherry pie.

7. Downstairs always cooks up fresh helpings of drama for Upstairs.

8. This episode features two dotty, chocolate-coated dames.

9. When a husband unused to kitchen duty attempts to cook dinner, he allows one pound of rice per person with the expected results.

10. After years on the force, the central character has become too portly to readily flee bullets, so he trades in his badge for a whisk.

Tortilla Soup (US 2001)

Directed by Maria Ripoll with Hector Elizando, Raquel Welsh, Elisabeth Pena, and Jacqueline Obradors.

An American version of Ang Lee's Eat Drink Man Woman, Tortilla Soup takes place in Los Angeles. The Mexican born father of three American daughters has lost his zest for life and his sense of taste like master chef Chu before him. He perfunctorily whips up traditional Mexican dishes like grilled cactus, fish in banana leaves, squash flower soup, and candied pumpkin, his aspiring chef daughter creates nouvelle dishes like lamb tamarindo on cabbage leaves and quinoa with Romesco sauce. Romantic troubles and the conflict between traditional vs. modern ways are thrown into the olla, yet everyone comes out happy in their personal lives and career choices. The film menus were created and styled by famed LA chefs Susan Fenniger and Mary Sue Milliken. Food preparation scenes don't get better than these. The DVD of the film includes recipes, so I've just suggested this as a light, easily prepared Mexican American lunch that requires no chef skills.

California Sangria
Guacamole Stuffed Tomatoes
Tortilla Soup
Porcupine Cookies

California Sangria

One part orange juice
One part grapefruit juice
One part sparkling water
3 parts red Spanish wine or try a California Grenache
For a white Sangria use:
3 parts Portuguese vinho verde, or you could substitute a sauvignon Blanc to be Californian

Blend and garnish with slice limes, lemons, oranges, and grapefruits.

Guacamole Stuffed Tomatoes

One clove garlic
2 large, ripe avocados
Salt to taste
Chopped cilantro to taste
Cherry tomatoes, halved

1. Coarsely mash the avocados.
2. Add the garlic, salt, and cilantro
3. Scoop the guacamole on the tomato halves and serve as hors d'oeuvres.

Tortilla Soup

6 corn tortillas, cut into one inch strips or in a clinch, thick packaged tortilla chips
¼ cup olive oil
1 small onion, chopped
2 cloves garlic, finely chopped
1 medium Anaheim, poblanos or jalapeno or chipotle chile, seeded and chopped
4 cups chicken broth or homemade chicken stock
1 can (14.5 oz) diced tomatoes, undrained
½ t coarse salt
1½ cups shredded cooked chicken

Garnish
1 ripe medium avocado, peeled and sliced
½ cup shredded Monterey Jack cheese or Cacique or other Chihuahua cheese
Chopped fresh cilantro
1 lime, cut into wedges

1. Heat oil in saucepan.
2. Fry the strips of tortillas until crispy; disregard this step if using packaged.

3. In the remaining oil fry the onion 2 minutes until soft. If using packaged reduce the amount of oil by half.
4. Add garlic and chili; cook 2 to 3 minutes Stir in broth, tomatoes and salt.
5. Heat to boiling.
6. Reduce heat; cover and simmer 15 minutes.
7. Add chicken and heat through.
8. Serve and garnish with tortilla strips, avocado, cheese, cilantro and a squirt of lime.

These sweet treats are more candy than cookie. Kids love them no matter what.

Porcupine Cookies

One cup pecans, walnuts, pine nuts, chopped hazelnuts or slivered almonds
2½ cups shredded sweet coconut
½ cup chopped dried apricots
½ cup semisweet morsels, chopped7 oz. sweetened condensed milk

1. Heat oven to 325.
2. Combine ingredients.
3. Grease or line a cookie sheet with parchment.
4. Place 2 T scoops of batter onto tray.
5. Flatten until about 2 inches in diameter.
6. Bake ten minutes or until coconut is golden.
7. Cool on a rack.

Food that Isn't Food Trivia Quiz

1. Under penalty of death, a comic duo is forced to make a shipboard breakfast for a deranged sea captain. They make bacon and eggs that are really shoe leather and a zipper.

2. Should this film be re-titled "Dog-Do Afternoon? "

3. Scatological dining off a silver platter.

4. Charlie Chaplin eats his boot.

5. Instead of filet of sole, a comic trio serves up the sole of a boot fished from the sea.

6. A documentary about a famous German filmmaker and what he eats.

Married to the Mob?

Films about the mafia rarely fail to incorporate food scenes. No matter how dastardly the doings depicted may be, food is bountiful and dining is of utmost importance to the mob members, whether they are eating surrounded by family at home, among fellow gangsters at restaurants, or even while incarcerated.

Gangster Grub Trivia Quiz

1. A bookie/restaurateur with mob connections weighs handing over the family restaurant to his celebrity chef son.

2. Whaddaya want a leg or a wing?" laughs one mobster to another while cutting up a body.

3. It doesn't matter how much cocaine goes up their noses, they're still fussy about what goes into their gullets.

4. A wannabe gangster describes New York street food as " warm germs."

5. While being nursed after a severe injury, Eric Roberts complains that his non-Italian friend dares to feed him canned soup instead of homemade.

6. Poisoned canolli puts an end to a duplicitous "friend" of this mafia family.

7. Gangsters and high fashion mix at a of London restaurant.

Goodfellas

(US 1990)

Martin Scorcese's ever-prowling camera follows the education, career and ultimate crash and burn of a mob wise guy. Ray Liotta teams with pragmatic Robert DeNiro and volatile Joe Pesci in the ranks of dead-eyed don Paul Sorvino. It's so much fun, fun, fun, (aside from the occasional grave digging duty), that it plays like a recruitment film for organized crime. That is, until drugs undermine what little honor there is among these thieves.

In Goodfellas food and dining scenes ground the characters whose violence otherwise makes them seem inhuman. Food symbolizes everything from family love and tradition to the corruption of prison officials. Ray Liotta, as Henry Hill, is as high as a helicopter and engineering a huge drug deal, yet neither prevents him from micromanaging the preparation of his family's Sunday dinner. His drug-addled wife maintains her role of proper mother when she admonishes diners from feeding the dog at the table. When Hill and fellow mobsters are jailed, this doesn't prevent them from dining on lobster, drinking wine and Cutty Sark, and seasoning their "prison" grub with plenty of garlic.

Because Henry Hill, the real life goodfella on whose life the film is based, once worked as a cook and is a food lover, his actual eating habits and family favorites are depicted in the film. In real life, when offered immunity and the witness protection program, he worried that rather than real spaghetti and meat sauce he'd get noodles in catsup in whatever bland American town to which he was relocated. I'm not going to include his recipes here, because Henry Hill wrote his own cookbook cum memoir, which is actually a good basic cookbook

Cook any hearty Italian fare to accompany this film: you will get hungry!

The Godfather

(US 1972)

Francis Ford Coppola explores the dark underbelly of the American Dream in this epic chronicle of the Corleone crime family. As patriarch Marlon Brando nears death, a war for his turf explodes among rival gangs. Is the second generation of Corleones tough enough to meet the challenge? Shakespearean in scope, this film secured the star status of Al Pacino, Diane Keaton, Robert Duvall, James and Caan.

In Francis Coppola's Godfather films, the WASP fiancée, played by Diane Keaton, is introduced to the culture of her future husband's family through lasagna at Talia Shire's wartime wedding. Mobsters serve up leftovers while plotting sinister deeds. Sofia Coppola gets to know her lover while seductively kneading gnocchi dough. And poisoned canolli puts an end to a duplicitous family "friend." And then there are the ubiquitous oranges and orange juice that seems to appear just before someone meets an untimely fate.

Had Francis Ford Coppola filmed the Godfather Saga in the 2000's rather than the 1970's, he would probably have depicted more Italian American food. Not only has a food revolution taken place in America, but also Coppola himself, of all the directors in this book, is the most involved with food. A restaurateur with a restaurant in San Francisco's North Beach; he stages fundraisers for his homeless organization, cooking for the guests himself. He has become a vintner, producing California reds, whites, and a champagne called Sofia. And he created the Mammarella brand of pastas and sauces. There are several varieties from rooster combs to pasta shaped rather like a rose, and tomato sauces with various ingredients. Buy some and serve with a salad, crusty bread, and a Coppola wine. Following is one recipe that uses the haunting orange of the Godfather in a pasta dish.

The pungent rosemary, salty crisp pancetta, sweet and bitter marmalade, and sweet onions are a brilliant combo you've never tasted: do not be put off.

Pasta with Marmalade

Anna Imparato's recipe appeared in Food and Wine and is adapted here.

3 oz. finely chopped pancetta
1 medium onion, thinly sliced
2 t chopped fresh rosemary leaves
2 T orange marmalade
Salt and pepper
½ pound fusilli
3 T olive oil
¼ cup Parmesan

1. Heat the oil.
2. Brown the pancetta for about 4 minutes.
3. Add the onion and rosemary and sauté for 10 minutes.
4. Meantime, boil the pasta.
5. Add the marmalade and salt and pepper.
6. Toss the drained, cooked pasta into the pan with about ⅓ cup of the pasta water.
7. Add cheese and serve.

You can serve with either red or white wine.

CHAPTER FOUR

Nibbling from Novels:

Menus from Great Literary Films

The food scenes based upon novels are, in my opinion, the best food scenes in cinema. Novelists use the multitude of metaphors of food and dining in the same way that screenwriters do, but generally in much greater detail. Therefore the screenwriter who adapts a novel to screen often has pages of excellent and specific material with which to work, usually choosing the most visually compelling aspects of the original.

Nibbling from Novels Trivia Quiz

We know you're a film buff and well fed, but how well read are you?

How many films with food scenes can you name that are based upon novels or stories?

What are the original titles? Who is the author?

Fellini's Satyricon

(Italy 1969)

Directed by Federico Fellini with Hiram Keller, Martin Potter, and Capucine.

Loosely based on surviving fragments of a tale by the ancient Roman writer Petronius, Satyricon depicts the misadventures of two friends and their slave. The food scene, one of the most colorful in cinema, takes place at the home of the nouveau riche Trimalchio who, fancying himself a poet, declares to his guests:

"Nothing but bones; that's what we are
Death hustles us humans away
Today we are here and tomorrow we're not
So live and drink while you may."

He then serves them a feast as lacking in subtlety as his poetry. The first course is presented on twelve circular trays, which represent the signs of the zodiac. For Aries, chickpeas: over Taurus, a beefsteak; a pair of kidneys and testicles represent Gemini, while a garland of flowers serve for Cancer an African fig becomes Leo: a virgin sowbelly, Virgo, Libra is a pair of scales with a tart on one side, balanced by a cheesecake on the other side. Scorpio is a crawfish, a lobster is Capricorn, a goose is Aquarius and two mullets are Pisces. Spicy liquid gushes out the phalluses of the satyr-shaped gravy boats.

Trimalchio's guests are treated to the sight of a boar being gutted as they dine. More tastefully, it turns out the animal is already roasted: from his bowels fall an array of steaming sausages and savory blood puddings.

Trimalchio's feast is not easily duplicated in the modern American kitchen. Fear not! I offer a simpler menu using components of Trimalchio's feast and dishes popular in Ancient Rome.

The Menu

Figs in Anchovy Sauce
Garbanzo Soup
Fish in Pomegranate Juice
Cheesecake

Figs in Anchovy Sauce (Aries)

Plump, ripe figs, washed off with a damp cloth
Anchovy fillets or a dab of anchovy paste
5 T olive oil
1 T sherry vinegar
Pepper
Chopped Parsley

1. Chop the anchovies and mix a vinaigrette with the oil, vinegar, and pepper.
2. Due to the saltiness of the anchovies you won't need additional salt.
3. Slice figs into quarters and display on serving plates.
4. Spoon the sauce over them lightly and garnish with parsley.

Garbanzo Soup (Leo)

You can prepare this recipe at short notice because most of the ingredients can be kept on hand.

2 cans garbanzo beans from a can, pureed in a Cuisinart, food mill or blender
3 T olive oil
1 onion, chopped
1 celery stalk, diced
1 clove garlic, chopped
2 T tomato paste
1 bay leaf
2 sprigs sage

1 ½ cups beef or chicken stock
Parmesan cheese
Water

1. Sauté the onion and celery until soft.
2. Do not let the garlic brown sauté only until soft and golden.
3. Add the tomato paste and stir.
4. Add the stock and sieved garbanzos to the onion, garlic and tomato paste.
5. Add bay leaf, and sage.
6. Add a fair amount of salt and pepper.
7. Simmer.
8. Add water as needed to thin the soup to desired consistency.

Serve with a sprinkling of Parmesan.

A chilled dry sherry is best to cut the texture of this rich soup. The best of all Sherries for the table is Fino.

Fish in Pomegranate Juice (Pisces)

4 fillets of snapper or red mullet or orange roughy
4 T of olive oil
1 T red wine vinegar
2 garlic cloves, crushed
4 T of pomegranate juice with seeds for garnish
2 large pomegranate sections

1. Mix the olive oil, the red wine vinegar, and the garlic.
2. Marinate the fish fillets for an hour in this mixture.
3. Grill the fish lightly on both sides so that the fish is cooked on the outside, but still tender on the inside.
4. Place pomegranate sections on the grill.
5. You can use an outdoor or indoor grill or the grill in your oven.

6. Sprinkle the cooked fish with pomegranate juice and garnish with seeds and the sections of pomegranate that have been grilled along with the fillets

Cheesecake (Libra)

2 cups flour
2 egg yolks
1 stick chilled butter
A pinch of salt
2 T granulated sugar
3 T chilled water

1. Preheat oven to 350.
2. Combine the flour, salt, and sugar.
3. Add in the butter, cutting with two dinner knives.
4. When the dough resembles crumbs ad the yolks.
5. Use the water as needed to form a cohesive dough.
6. Form a ball.
7. Cover and refrigerate.

2 pounds whole milk ricotta cheese, drained with a cheesecloth or strainer overnight in the fridge
½ cup butter
3 eggs, separated
4 oz. citron
2 oz. pine nuts
6 T sugar
2 T liqueur such as Maraschino, Strega, or Amoretto)

1. Heat oven to 350.
2. Blend the egg yolks with the ricotta, citron, sugar, and liqueur.
3. Beat the egg whites until stiff.
4. Gently fold the whites into the cheese mixture.
5. Roll out the chilled dough into 2 round crusts, one large then the other.

6. Place the largest on the bottom of an 8 or 9 inch spring form pan.
7. Pour in the cheese mixture.
8. Cover with the smaller crusts and pinch the edges together.
9. Bake for fifty minutes on the top shelf of the oven.
10. Remove from the pan when completely cool.

To the Lighthouse

(UK 1983)

Directed by Colin Gregg based on the novel by Virginia Woolf, with Rosemary Harris, Michael Gough, and Kenneth Branagh.

The film recalls a family at their seaside holidays in the early 20th century. The mother is a nurturing, creative presence who presides lovingly over meals with family and guests (although the meals are actually prepared by the maid, Mildred)

This English summer meal is also perfect for a San Francisco summer dinner when seasonal ingredients are readily available but the foggy weather makes a hearty entrée appealing.

The Menu

English Style Salad
Bouef en Daube
Braised Peas and Lettuce
Rhubarb Pudding

English Style Salad

Greens of choice. Use the best and save any tired ones for the peas and lettuce dish
Dressing
The yolks of 2 hardboiled eggs, mashed
1 T oil
2 T vinegar

½ cup whipping cream
A pinch of cayenne
Salt and pepper to taste
Blend.

You can also purchase a bottled of English salad cream from an import store

"Mildred's masterpiece was Bouef en Daube. Everything depends upon being served up to the precise moment they are ready. The beef, the bay leaf, and the wine, all must be done to a turn."

Bouef en Daube

2 ½ lbs top round or brisket
¼ lb bacon
1 onion
4 cloves garlic
4 T good olive oil
1 cup good red wine
¼ cup dry vermouth
3 sprigs fresh thyme
1 large sprig of rosemary
1 bay leaf
A three inch strip of orange peel
1 T tomato paste
Salt
Fresh ground pepper
One half can or one half cup of pitted black olives

1. Preheat oven to 350.
2. Cut the meat into large stew size chunks.
3. Trim excess fat.
4. Chop the bacon.
5. Peel and chop the onions and garlic.
6. Heat the olive oil in a casserole.
7. Brown the bacon, garlic, and onion.
8. Be careful not to overcook.

9. Remove the onion, garlic, and bacon and put aside.
10. Brown the beef on all sides.
11. Return the bacon, onion, and garlic to the beef.
12. Add the vermouth, thyme, bay leaf, orange peel, and tomato paste. Season to taste.
13. Cook in the oven until the beef is tender, about two hours.
14. Add the olives and cook for thirty minutes more.

"An exquisite scent of olives and oil and juice rose from the great brown dish as Martha (with a little flourish) took the cover off."

Braised Peas and Lettuce

1 package of frozen peas or 2 pounds of fresh English pea pods
Lettuce eaves, perhaps red leaf
Heavy cream
3 scallions, cut diagonally into 3inch strips
Salt
Pepper
Fresh tarragon

1. Cook the peas according to package or shell the peas and boil the larger peas first because they are starchy and take longer to cook and then add the smaller peas later. Test for doneness. Times vary greatly depending on the size of the peas.
2. Drain off the water.
3. Add the lettuce and scallions
4. Heat until wilted.
5. Add a dash of cream, the tarragon, and salt and pepper to taste.

Rhubarb Pudding

½ lb. rhubarb, cut up
3 oz. of brown sugar and 4 additional oz.
The zest and juice of one orange
8 oz. of crushed macaroon crumbs
1 t cinnamon

1. Heat oven to 350.
2. Place the rhubarb, juice, zest, and sugar in a casserole and bake until soft, about 30 minutes.
3. Remove and put the oven up to 400.
4. Cool.
5. Melt the butter in a sauté pan.
6. Stir in the crumbs, the sugar, and the cinnamon and cook gently for about five minutes, being careful not to burn.
7. Cover the rhubarb with the crumbs.
8. Bake for fifteen minutes at 400.
9. Serve hot, warm, or cold with ice cream, whipped cream, or plain yogurt.

Babette's Feast

(Denmark 1987)

Directed by Gabriel Axel based on Isak Dinesen's story "The Supper at Ellsinore."

With Asta Anderson, Therese Christensen, and Stephane Audran as Babette.

In a remote Danish village, two plain-living spinster sisters renounce their own dreams to carry on the ministry of their late father. In the course of their good works the pair take in a Frenchwoman who has escaped from the turmoil of war torn France of the 1870's.

Babette's self sacrifice is as great as the sisters. She lives in worse circumstances than they, having only herself for company, sleeping in an outbuilding, eating their humble fare with none of her dreary daily experience buoyed by self-righteous religious fervor.

What follows redefines the term "soul food" in what may be the greatest food film of all time. The devout diners from "The Supper at Elsinore" have promised not to comment on their meal, so the reader doesn't learn as much about the best meal ever prepared as might be wished. But happily the filmmaker, Gabriel Axel, fills in culinary blanks unforgettably.

Baroness Karin Blixen, pen-named Isak Dinesen, was an accomplished cook herself and even trained her African servant to be a great cook, yet there is very little food in her works. When she was dying of syphilis in her old age Blixen lived on grapes, oysters, and champagne.

This is the fare that the pious, sensually unaware, sisters of "Babette's Feast" lived on before Babette created her memorable meal.

Bread and Ale Soup
Boiled Cod
Coffee
Cookies

This is the cinematic Babette's idea of a good meal:

Turtle Soup with Profiteroles
Sherry
Blinis Demidoff with Caviar and Crème Fraiche
Champagne
Cailles en sarcophages
Baba au Rum with fruit
Pineapple, Papayas, Chestnuts, Figs
Cheeses
Endive Salad
Red Wine
Coffee

Babette's menu, while delicious is old-fashioned, labor intensive, expensive, and includes an endangered species. I've updated and simplified her feast so you needn't toil all day in the kitchen. And because some of the dishes or their components can be prepared in advance, unlike poor Babette you can sit down with your guests to eat!

The Menu

Bread and Ale Soup
Amontillado Sherry
Blinis with Caviar and Crème Fraiche
Champagne such as Veuve Cliquot, Perrier-Jouet or Pol Roger
Quail on Pastry Shells with Pate in Port Sauce
French Red Wine
Endive Salad
Babas au Rhum from your bakery
Fresh seasonal fruit with matched cheeses
Coffee

Bread and Ale Soup

Because no one serves turtle soup any longer I thought it might be fun to commence this feast with a sampling of the bread soup that was the sisters' daily fare. What a contrast to the meal that will follow! The sisters' "Ollebrod" was made from stale rye bread and ale. But I offer you a more palatable bread soup.

2 medium yellow onions, chopped
2 T butter
One loaf brown bread torn into squares then soaked for three hours or longer in:
1 cup milk or one cup ale, or any Danish or American beer
2 cups beef or chicken stock
½ pint sour cream
2 T parsley, chopped for garnish
2 T green onions, chopped for garnish

1. Melt the butter in a saucepan.
2. Add the onions and cook until they are soft and transparent.

3. Puree the softened bread in a blender or food processor. (You can pound it in a bowl with a wooden spoon until smooth as Babette did.)
4. Add the broth to the onions and then stir in the bread mixture.
5. Heat until very smooth.
6. Serve the bread soup with a voluminous dash of sour cream and sprinkle with parsley and chives.

Blinis with Caviar

The blinis may be made in advance and reheated in the oven before serving.

⅓ cup of milk, warmed
A package of yeast
1 T sugar
1 cup buckwheat flour
1 cup pastry flour
4 eggs, whisked
Melted butter
Caviar-The nicest you can afford
Crème fraiche or sour cream

1. Combine the yeast and warmed milk in a mixing bowl, stirring until the yeast dissolves and bubbles.
2. Stir in the sugar.
3. Add the flours and eggs to the milk mixture and blend.
4. Cover with a kitchen towel.
5. Let sit in a warm place.
6. Melt butter to coat the bottom of a crepe pan.
7. Pour about three Tablespoonsful of batter into the pan shaking to coat the pan with batter.
8. Cook the blini until browned and bubbly then turn over with a two-pronged fork.
9. Cook until browned on the second side.
10. (Often the first crepe doesn't turn out so well. This is normal. Throw it away and proceed. It gets easier.)

11. Reserve cooked blinis on a hot plate under a towel while preparing the others.

Serve with a dribble of melted butter, a spoonful of caviar, and a dollop of crème fraiche. You can set up the plates for your guests or provide the blini makings on the table and let them help themselves.

If personal taste or budget doesn't include caviar use smoked salmon instead.

Quails on Pastry Shells with Port

Pepperidge Farm pastry shells or vol au vents from a bakery
4 frozen quail, defrosted
One package prepared glace du viande or 1 ½ cups veal stock
½ cup (or more to taste) port wine
Pate de foie gras with truffles, divided into four portions
One black truffle, cut into four (optional)
4 T butter, plus 2 additional T cold butter cut into ½ inch cubes
5 T arrowroot dissolved in ⅓cup water
Salt and pepper

1. Bake the pastry shells according to instructions. Or use pastry sheets, cutting them into coffin shaped rectangles large enough to entomb your quail.
2. Put aside while cooling.
3. When baked, cut out a rectangular section, like a sarcophagus lid, with a sharp knife and put in fois gras, paté de fois gras and/or truffles.
4. Then place the quail in a baking dish in a 500 degree oven.
5. Meanwhile add 1 ½ cups water to one package glace du viande or 1 ½ cups veal stock in a saucepan and cook over medium heat reduce by half until the mixture is thick.
6. Melt 4 T butter in a heavy pan.
7. Brown the salted and peppered quail on all sides until evenly golden colored. Don't let the pan burn.
8. Place the browned birds in a roasting pan in the oven for 8 to 10 minutes.

9. While the birds are roasting, add ½ cup port to the browning pan and deglaze, scraping sides of pan.
10. Add the reduced stock to this and thicken about ten minutes.
11. If when a test bird is pierced the juice trickling out is bloody roast for three more minutes.
12. When the juice tests clear, remove.
13. Do not overcook.
14. When the birds are cooked place them on a heated platter.
15. Add 2 T cold, cubed butter and whisk into the stock and port mixture.
16. Season with salt and pepper to taste.
17. Place a hot bird on each shell and pour the sauce over it.
18. Serve immediately.

Endive Salad

12 fresh, firm Belgian endive bulbs
Champagne vinegar
Good virgin olive oil
Salt and pepper
Chives, chopped fine

1. Slice the endive lengthwise into bite size pieces.
2. Mix the vinegar, salt, and pepper and a handful of minced chives in the bottom of a salad bowl.
3. Add olive oil and whip until opaque.
4. Toss in the endives and lightly coat them with dressing. Place on salad plates and serve.

Baba au Rhum

Buy a baba or individual babas at the store or order them on line.

Seasonal Fruits and Cheeses

Because fruits were not flown daily worldwide in Babette's era, each of the fruits she served to her incredulous, but under-reacting diners would have been exotic to them. Your guests will have eaten many varieties of fruit so you need not impress them with exoticism. Simply choose any ripe fruit in season.

When buying cheeses ask the dealer to recommend a cheese that would pair well with the fruit you intend to serve.

In autumn serve red, purple or green grapes along with purple or green figs and apples. Purple grapes and ripe Brie or Roquefort go beautifully together. Italian mascarpone goes well with figs. Apples pair well with any sharp cheddar.

In spring always-popular strawberries are plentiful. Lightly sweetened crème fraiche or honeyed ricotta pairs wonderfully with spring strawberries and so does a fresh goat cheese.

In summer, stone fruits such as plums, nectarines, peaches, and cherries are at their best. Serve any of them with a creamy blue cheese.

In winter, apples and pears are plentiful. Again apples call for cheddars while pears are delicious with Italian Gorgonzola or French Roquefort.

Coffee

"Coffee, according to the women of Denmark, is to the body what religion is to the soul."

Anna Karenina

The story of Anne Karenina by Leo Tolstoy has been depicted in film and for television dozens of times by Russian, French, Italian, American, and British directors You may have seen some of the classic American and British versions.

1935 saw Greta Garbo, Frederic March, and Maureen O'Sullivan. In 1948 Vivien Leigh played with Ralph Richardson. One version worth watching is the 1997 British version with Sophie Morceau. A new Russian version premiered in 2005.

In Anna Karenina, food is used to illustrate the politics of the characters, as in the case of Levin, who rejects the French style cuisine favored by the aristocracy in Imperial Russia, such as turbot Beaumarchais, for simpler pleasant food, such as buckwheat kasha and cabbage soup. Levin is right. White cabbage soup and porridge à la russe or kasha make a delicious, hearty, and inexpensive meal. Prepare kasha as directed on package.

The Menu

White Cabbage Soup
Kasha
Russian Rye
Russian Tea Cakes
Russian Caravan Tea with Jam

Alexis Astaff's Cheating Shchi

2 large yellow onions, thinly sliced
12 oz. sauerkraut, tinned, drained
2 small cans beef or chicken broth or four cups broth from bouillon cubes, or four cups fresh beef stock
2 medium potatoes, peeled and cut matchstick size

You may add parsnips, carrots, turnips, rutabagas or kohlrabi, also julienned. Or you can use fresh white cabbage sliced thin.

A dash of cider vinegar
4 pepper corns
Fresh dill

1. Toss in a pot.
2. Cover and cook until vegetables are tender.
3. Serve with sour cream.

Like Water for Chocolate

(1992) Mexico

Alfonso Arua directed Lumi Cavazos, Marco Leonardi, and Regina Torne. His wife, Laura Esquivel, penned the novel, set in early 1900's Mexico. A young woman repressed by a cold mother gains power through cooking by inflicting pain, providing pleasure, or doling out punishment. Dishes range from the romantic and delicate Quail with Rose Petals, to dishes used to exact revenge on the digestive systems of enemies. (I don't include any of the latter.) Recipes are included in the novel itself.

Turkey Mole
Hot Chocolate

Hot Chocolate

4 oz bittersweet chocolate, grated
1 ancho chile, seeded, then cut into six pieces
1 cinnamon stick
One quart milk

1. Heat the milk with the chile and cinnamon.
2. Remove from heat. Remove the chile and cinnamon stick.
3. Return to heat and add the chocolate.

Turkey Mole (or Chicken)

A nun from Pueblo, who hoped to impress a visiting viceroy, invented this Mexican favorite. I'm sure he was impressed. The ingredients have evolved over the years. Versions use everything from bread to bananas. I have included a simplified version using either turkey or chicken. Turkey is more authentic, but harder to handle, as it can dry out. Chicken is perfectly delicious and easier for the novice cook. This is Mole 101.

3 cloves garlic
1 green pepper

2 tomatoes
2 oz. unsweetened baking chocolate
1 t salt
1 t pepper
1 t chili powder
1 t cinnamon
1 onion, chopped
1 turkey escallops or several chicken pieces
1 quart chicken broth
Shelled pumpkin seeds

1. If using turkey gently poach the escallops in boiling chicken broth that has been brought to a simmer once the escallops are added. Be careful not to overcook.
2. Brown the chicken on all sides if using chicken, then place in a baking dish.
3. Pulse the garlic, pepper, tomatoes, onions, chopped chocolate, and all the spices in a food processor until pureed.
4. Pour over the chicken.
5. Bake for 30 minutes at 350.
6. If using turkey let sit in sauce for an hour then gently reheat.
7. Toss with pumpkin seeds before serving.

How Green Was My Valley

(US 1944)

Directed by John Ford based on the novel by Richard Llewellyn with Walter Pidgeon, Maureen O'Hara, and Roddy McDowell.

This nostalgic memoir of a Welsh mining family in the early twentieth century becomes in the film a sanitized version of mining life where the houses are spotless, the air is pure, (where does all that coal dust get to?) and the miners wouldn't dream of getting up to anything so disloyal as joining a union.

In Richard Llewellyn's novel, *How Green Was My Valley,* the following excerpt indicates just how much the director and screenwriter gain from the novelist's imagination. "In front of him were the chickens either boiled or roast, or a duck or a turkey or a goose, whatever was the time of year. The potatoes mashed, boiled and roast, and the cabbage or cauliflower and peas or beans and when the weather was good all of them together. When we sat down with me in Mam's lap, my father would ladle out of the cauldron thin leek soup, with a big lump of ham in it that showed its rind as it turned over through the steam when the ladle came out brimming over."

The Menu

Potato Leek & Ham Soup
Home Baked Bread
Apple Pudding
Toffee
Tea

For a simple family meal prepare this hearty soup and the oatmeal bread from Alice's Restaurant. Serve with hot tea, ale, or Blackthorne's sparkling apple cider.

Potato, Leek & Ham Soup

2 pounds of potatoes
2 heaping T of butter
6 cups milk or 3 of milk and 3 of water or 3 cups milk and 3 cups chicken stock
Chopped chives
2 leeks
1 cup cream
¼ pound ham with the bone
Salt and pepper

1. Melt the butter and sweat the sliced leeks in it.
2. Do not let them brown.
3. Add the peeled and sliced potatoes.

4. Season to taste and then add the milk and water and stock or your combination thereof. Cover and cook for one hour.
5. Then force the liquid through a food mill or food processor.
6. Add cream and reheat gently.
7. Serve with chopped chives and diced ham.

Apple Pudding

1 lb apples, peeled, cored, and cut into small chunks
1 oz butter or 2 T
1 oz sugar or 1 ½ T
1 small lemon rind, grated

1. Melt the butter in a saucepan.
2. Add the apples and sugar.
3. Cook slowly, stirring occasionally until the apples are soft and thick.
4. Remove from heat and add the peel.
5. Pour into a 2 quart baking dish.

1 egg, beaten
1 oz or 2 T butter
1 oz. or 4 T flour
2½ cups milk
1 oz or 3 T sugar

1. Melt the butter in a saucepan.
2. Add the flour and cook gently without browning, for two minutes.
3. Add the milk while stirring and bring to a boil.
4. Simmer for two minutes. Remove from heat and stir in sugar.
5. Pour over apples.

2 oz brown sugar
½ t cinnamon
½ T butter

1. Mix. Crumble over pudding.
2. Place in the broiler and heat until sugar is caramelized.
3. Serve pudding hot or cold.

Toffee

2 cups sugar
1½ cups dark corn syrup
1½ cups cream
⅓ cup butter
1 t vanilla or rum

1. Place sugar, syrup, and cream into a saucepan
2. Blend over low heat until the mixture comes to a boil.
3. Dip a candy thermometer into the liquid and allow to boil without stirring until it attains a temperature of 244 degrees.
4. Remove from heat and add the butter.
5. Reheat to 252.
6. Add flavoring.
7. Pour into a 7 by 11 inch pan that has been lined with wax paper.
8. Mark into squares with a knife before the toffee hardens.
9. When hardened, cut and wrap each piece in waxed paper.

The Dead
(USA 1987)

John Huston directed his daughter Angelica Huston with Donald McCann, and Dan O' Herlihy in the screenplay by his son Tony Huston.

Much of James Joyce's *"The Dead"* revolves around the Christmas seasonal meal of Epiphany. Joyce tells us every component of the meal.

John Huston left little out in his recreation of the era, season, country, and social class of the characters.

The Film Menu

Roast Goose
Limerick Ham with Crust Crumbs
Spiced Beef
Whole Potatoes
Plum Pudding (see *A Christmas Carol*)
Blancmange with Berry Jam
Figs
Dried Apricots
Almonds
Celery
Raisins
Oranges and Apples
Green Pears
Mineral water
Port
Punch
Lemonade
Guinness
Sherry

My Menu

Apple, Celery and Hazelnut Salad
Spiced Beef Stew
Boiled Potatoes
Blancmange and Berry Jam
Pears with Irish Cashel Blue Cheese
Irish Soda Bread and Butter
Guinness

This fresh and crunchy winter salad is easy to make

Apple, Celery, and Hazelnut Salad

½ celery stalk per person, washed and sliced on the diagonal
½ green apple per person, cored, cut into eights and sliced
Salt and pepper
4 T olive oil, salad oil, or hazel nut oil or any combination thereof
4 T apple cider vinegar
8 T chopped hazelnuts
Lettuce leaves

1. Whisk the vinegar, oil, salt and pepper together.
2. Toss the celery and apples in the dressing until coated.
3. Served over crisp lettuce leave.
4. Garnish with chopped hazelnuts.

Since traditional Christmastime Irish spiced beef calls for saltpeter and takes up to a week to prepare and several hours to cook, I've taken the flavors and created a flavorful stew you can make and serve the same day.

Spiced Beef Stew

Serves 8
2 pounds beef chuck, brisket, or rump cut into one inch cubes
2 large onions, sliced thinly
2 T cooking oil
A pinch of mace (optional)
½ t whole allspice
1 T juniper berries
1 t whole peppercorns
1 bay leaf
A sprig each of parsley, sage, and thyme
2 whole cloves
2 cloves of garlic

2 rounded t brown sugar
½ t salt
½ t pepper
2 cups beef stock, canned,
1 cup stout
8 carrots, peeled and chunked
2 T minced parsley

1. Put the oil in a Dutch oven and heat.
2. Brown the meat cubes on each side until no pink parts remain.
3. Remove the meat from the pot and toss in the onions
4. Fry until soft and transparent.
5. Add the beef back to the pot.
6. Toss in a bouquet garni comprised of the allspice, juniper berries, peppercorns, bay leaf, parsley, sage, thyme, and cloves wrapped and tied in cheesecloth.
7. Add the liquids, sugar, and carrots.
8. Cover and simmer until the meat is tender or place in a medium oven and cook for about two to two and a half hours.
9. Sprinkle with minced parsley, test seasoning, and serve with boiled potatoes.

Pears with Cashel Blue Cheese

4 ripe, unblemished pears
8 T Cashel blue cheese or you can use Gorgonzola instead
Mint leaves

1. Cut attractive ripe pears in half and scoop out the seeds and core.
2. Fill the hole with softened cheese.
3. Return to the fridge.
4. Serve cheese side down garnished with mint leaves.

Blancmange and Berry Jam

In Ireland this dish is made with Irish moss or Carrageen seaweed. For the sake of ease I suggest you use packaged gelatin instead.

8 oz. blanched almonds
¾ cup scalded milk

1. Whiz the almonds and milk in a blender or processor briefly.
2. Drain over a sieve lined with cheesecloth.
3. Mash the almonds with the back of a wooden spoon or squeeze through the cheesecloth.

1 packet gelatin
¼ cup water

1. Dissolve the gelatin in the water.

One cup whipping cream
½ cup sugar
2 t almond extract or to taste
Berry jam
Mint leaves or holly looks very pretty as garnish

1. Whip cream and sugar in Cuisinart or with a mixer.
2. Combine the almond milk, gelatin mixture and cream.
3. Blend and add:

2 t almond extract or to taste

Serve with late harvest Sauvignon Blanc or similar wine.

The Leopard

(Italy 1963)

Directed by Luchino Visconti with Burt Lancaster, Claudia Cardinale, and Alain Delon

In the classic di Lampedusa novel, The Leopard, depictions of food recreate a highly specific atmosphere. Specialties such as the Triumph of Gluttony cake place the locale in Sicily, and dishes that have lost their popularity today, such as chaud-froids and galantines, place the action in the 19th century. The elaborate, labor-intensive feast could only be created for the very wealthy.

"...coralline lobsters boiled alive, waxy chaud-froids of veal, steely-hued fish immersed in sauce, turkeys gilded by the oven's heat, rosy foie gras under gelatin armor, boned woodcock reclining on amber toast decorated with their own chopped insides, dawn-tinted galantine and a dozen other cruel, colored delights. At the end of the table two monumental silver tureens held clear soup the tint of burnt amber. . Huge sorrel babas, Mont Blancs snowy with whipped cream, cakes speckled with white almonds and green pistachio nuts, hillocks of chocolate covered pastry, brown and rich as the topsoil of a Catanian plain from which, in fact, through many a twist and turn they had come, pink ices, champagne ices, coffee ices, all parfaits, crystallized cherries, notes of yellow pineapple and those cakes called "triumphs of gluttony" of green pistachio paste, shameless " virgins" cakes, shaped like breasts. Don Fabrizio asked for some of these and, as he held them in his plate, looked like a profane caricature of St. Agatha claiming her own sliced-off breasts. "Why ever didn't the Holy Office forbid these cakes when it had the chance? St. Agatha's sliced-off teats sold by convents, devoured at dances!

My Menu

Turkey Stuffed with Fruit and Parmesan
Chocolate Chestnut Dessert
Timbale

This turkey "gilded by the oven's heat" is a change for Americans accustomed to a traditional bread and sage stuffing. The ingredients create a rich and sweet filling excellent for holiday dinners.

Tacchina Ripiena~Stuffed Turkey

One 8 to 10 pound turkey
8 T butter
1 sprig of fresh or dried sage, whole
1 sprig of fresh or dried rosemary
½ pound fresh skinned chestnuts, or dried chestnuts, soaked
½ pound dried prunes
¼ pound bacon, chopped finely
3 crisp green apples, peeled and chopped
3 ripe pears, peeled and chopped
12 walnut halves chopped
5 T grated Parmesan cheese
1 t salt
¼ t black pepper
¼ t grated nutmeg
2 eggs lightly beaten
1 cup dry white Italian wine

1. Preheat the oven to 375.
2. Rub the turkey inside and out with salt and pepper.
3. Chop the heart and liver of the turkey and add all the stuffing ingredients.
4. Stuff the bird loosely.
5. Place on a roasting pan and sew shut as with any turkey. Smear with butter and sprinkle with salt, and chopped sage and rosemary.
6. Allow 20 to 25 minutes per pound.
7. Baste every so often.

I serve this scrumptious dessert every Christmas.

Monte Bianco-Chestnut Dessert

1 pound chestnuts
Milk enough to cover chestnuts
Pinch of salt
6 oz. of chocolate bits or chopped bittersweet chocolate
¼ cup rum
2 cups cold whipping cream
2 T sugar

1. Boil the chestnuts slowly in the milk until the milk is absorbed.
2. Melt the chocolate over a double boiler.
3. Puree the chestnuts in a food mill or food processor. Add the chocolate and the rum.
4. Put through a food mill again, directly onto the platter on which it will be served.
5. Try to create a mountain shape. If you're not careful the mound will look more cow pie than mountain peak.
6. If you don't have a food mill you can pipe it out through a pastry bag.
7. Whip the cream stiff.
8. Add the sugar.
9. Place cream on the top of the mountain to make it look like snow.
10. You can decorate with toy trees if desired.

To use fresh chestnuts:

1. Score the nuts with a sharp knife on their flat side being careful not to cut the flesh.
2. Boil in a large pot of water for twenty-five minutes.
3. Peel immediately, both the outer shell and the tough inner skin.
4. Chop and puree.

Making this rich, old-fashioned dish can be an all day affair or made from leftovers and packaged ingredients, an hour's labor. Either result is unusually delicious. You can also do without the crusts and make a marvelous pasta dish.

Timbale

4 sheets of frozen puff paste, thawed (or make your own)
½ cup Marsala (sherry will do in a pinch)
2 carrots peeled, and diced
¼ cup yellow onion, diced
2 slices ham, diced (you can also use some Prosciutto or leftover pork instead)
1 whole boneless, skinless chicken breast diced (you can use leftover roast chicken too)
¼ cup diced chicken liver (optional)
2 hard-boiled eggs, chopped.
4 pints veal or beef broth reduced until two pints are left (you can use chicken broth in a pinch)
Cinnamon
Cloves or ground cloves
1 ½ T tomato paste
Truffles or sliced mushrooms
2 T flour
1 T butter
Salt and pepper
1 package penne rigate, cooked and drained (you can use leftover)
Grated Parmesan
1 egg, separated and white and yolk whisked, with a dash of water added to yolk
Olive oil

1. Roll out the pastry to 1/8 inch.
2. Place one half in the bottom of a spring form pan.
3. Cover the crust with foil and a layer of rice or raw beans and bake for 15 minutes, at 350.

4. Remove the foil and beans or rice and bake another 10 minutes.
5. In a sauté pan of hot olive oil, fry the onions until golden, the carrots until crisp tender, the ham, the chicken until browned and the chicken livers until browned, and the mushrooms until soft if using.
6. In the meantime prepare the pasta according to the package
7. Combine the sautéed ingredients.
8. Add the Marsala and toss.
9. Melt the butter and add the flour, cooking for one minute. Form a roux. Add the broth and heat until thick.
10. Add the tomato paste, cinnamon and cloves to taste.
11. Salt and pepper.
12. Add the pasta and Parmesan and toss
13. Add all to the pastry.
14. Cover with chopped or sliced boiled eggs and the truffle if using.
15. Cover with remaining crust pierced with a fork here and there.
16. Seal the cooked and raw crusts with egg white.
17. Paint the top crust with egg yolk.
18. Bake 45 to 50 minutes until risen and golden crisp.

Jean De Florette

(France 1986)

Directed by Claude Berri from the novel by Marcel Pagnol with Yves Montand, Gerard Depardieu, and Daniel Auteuil.

Gerard Depardieu plays the title character, an idealistic city dweller trying to make a go of it as a rabbit farmer in the hardscrabble hills of early 20th century Provence, his ancestral home. Unbeknownst to him, local landowners covet his property and will stop at nothing to force him to surrender his claim. The film employs the components of epic tragedy and is equally riveting.

As sad a story as is Jean de Florette, its abundant charm evokes the summer heat and delectable fragrances of southern France. Watching it might well make you hungry. Fresh rabbits, plump squabs, fat snails, ripe figs, almonds, apricots, grapes, and the local red and white wines all may tantalize the viewer of this film. Although specific dishes are not addressed in this film, I've devised a simple Provençal menu for your guests.

Set your table with colorful Provençal tablecloth and napkins. As a centerpiece feature a vase of blooming French lavender or if you dare… a huge bouquet of rich, red carnations. As background music play the bucolic, sprightly, yet sporadically mournful "Songs of the Auvergne" by Canteloube.

This is my favorite meal from any film.

My Menu

Aperitif such as Pastis
Escargots Provencal
Soupe au Pistou
Crusty French bread
Honeyed Squab
Harvest Fruit Tart
Or a Cherry Clafouti
Figs, Grapes, Apricots
Domaine Terres Blanches or Cotes de Provences wines

Escargots Provençal

4 T sweet butter
2 large garlic cloves
2 T chopped basil
Salt and pepper to taste
One can Roma tomatoes, chopped
1 T olive oil
1 small shallot
1 t herbes de Provence
24 to 36 snails drained

1. Mash or process the basil, butter, and garlic until smooth.
2. In a skillet heat the oil and add shallot.
3. Sauté until soft.
4. Add tomatoes, herbes de Provence and cook until thick, about 20 minutes.
5. Spoon into ramekins.
6. Divide the snails and place them on the tomato sauce.
7. Top with basil butter.
8. These can be made ahead and kept chilled.
9. Broil or bake at 450 until hot.
10. Serve with bread.

Soupe au Pistou

2 medium leeks sliced crosswise
6 oz. yellow onion finely sliced
6 oz. of carrots finely sliced
12 oz. of potatoes peeled quartered and sliced
10 oz. of summer squash peeled and coarsely diced
1 pound white beans (optional)
A few celery leaves, three sprigs of parsley, a bay leaf, a few sprigs of thyme (bouquet garni)
2 ½ quarts of water
6 oz. of green beans cut into inch long pieces
2 small zucchini
1 cup elbow macaroni

Pistou
4 large cloves of garlic
1 bunch of fresh basil
Salt
Pepper
1 cup freshly grated Parmesan
1 ripe tomato seeded and diced
1 ¼ cups good olive oil

1. Add the leeks, onions, potatoes, squash, beans, bouquet garni and water and cook covered for ½ hour in a large soup pot.
2. Add the beans, zucchini, and macaroni and cook for fifteen minutes.
3. Test the green beans and macaroni for doneness.
4. While the soup is cooking, pound the garlic, basil, and salt and pepper in a mortar and pestle or in your processor.
5. Work in the cheese until a thick paste forms.
6. Add the tomatoes.
7. Add more olive oil and more tomato until the paste becomes fluid.
8. Serve the soup hot and let everyone add the pistou according to personal taste.

Honeyed Squab

Marinate 2 hours to overnight:

4 squabs (or game hens) in
¾ cup lavender (or any) honey,
½ cup white wine
¼ cup olive oil
4 sprigs fresh thyme, stemmed
Sea salt and fresh ground pepper to taste

1. Broil five minutes or more each side.
2. Leave pink and tender.
3. For game hen, which is larger, broil until the juice runs clear when the bird is poked with a fork.
4. Let either bird rest five minutes before serving.

Harvest Fruit Tart

2 quarts of cherries, pitted
10 apricots, pitted and halved
15 whole almonds

Crust
1⅓ cup flour
⅔ cup sweet butter
1 egg yolk
1 t sugar
⅓ plus cup cold water

1. Combine the flour and sugar.
2. Blend with the butter until it is oatmeal like consistency.
3. Add the egg and just enough water to form a ball.
4. Roll out and place in a nine-inch pie plate.

Cream Mixture
1 cup sugar
9 T flour
8 T cream
3 T sweet butter
1 egg

1. Preheat the oven to 350.
2. Combine above ingredients and blend until smooth.
3. Line piecrust with the fruit.
4. Pour the cream mixture over it.
5. Sprinkle with two T sugar.
6. Bake for 30 to 35 minutes.

Manon of the Spring

(France 1986)

Claude Berri directed Emmanuelle Beart, Yves Montand, and Daniel Auteuil

This sequel to Jean de Florette is the revenge story of Jean's daughter, Manon, who has become a shepherdess but still must deal with the machinations of the townspeople. It is interesting to note that the repugnant Ugolin played by Daniel Auteuil and the sylphlike Emmanuelle Beart married in real life.

My Menu

Goat cheese
Crisp French bread
Olives or a fig and olive spread or tapenade
Wine
Mineral water
Salad

Our Manon spends most of her days afield so our menu needs no cooking. Serve any variety of goat cheese, crisp French bread, olives or a fig and olive spread or tapenade, icy white wine, Perrier water, and a salad of mixed greens with good olive oil, sea salt, fresh ground pepper, and lemon juice or tarragon vinegar.

If you enjoy "Jean de Florette" you might also like the charming and not at all tragic "My Father's Glory" and "My Mother's Castle", two films by Yves Robert based on the memoirs of Marcel Pagnol, the author of Jean de Florette. These gentle family stories are nostalgic, but not overly sentimental. For accompaniment any of the foods from the "Jean de Florette" menu or from "A Sunday in the Country" would be appropriate.

CHAPTER FIVE

Dinner Rush (US 2002)

Dishes from Restaurant Flicks

Everyone has dined at a restaurant whether it was a noisy family visit to MacDonald's or a sedate dinner at the chic showcase of a celebrity chef. Yet even for people who eat out daily, the inner workings of a restaurant may be a complete mystery.

Restaurant films expose that mysterious pre-democratic world of the eatery. The executive chef, head chef, sous chefs, line cooks, prep cooks, and vendors dwell in the fortified kingdom of the kitchen. In the fiefdom at the front of the house, managers, maitre d's, hosts, waiters, busboys, and bartenders reside. The customers come to pay homage or to request favors; they range from the royal friends of the chef, to the courtier-like regulars, to food critics practicing their own form of espionage, to the peasantry; tourists, families, and couples on first dates. We instantly recognize the front-of-the-house types: the haughty waiter who makes you want to crawl under the table and the friendly waiter who acts a though he's known you since kindergarten. We are familiar with the preposterously demanding customer as well as the diner who, in an urgent show of democratic feeling, bores the wait staff through incessant chatter in an attempt to "make them feel like people instead of servants". Given these intersecting social circles the restaurant is a mirror of society. The emotions reflected in a restaurant are as hot as the pizza oven and as cold as the walk in refrigerator.

This may be a reason there's a smorgasbord of restaurant movies. Actors portray waiters exceedingly well: their camaraderie and rivalry, their peevishness and snobbery, their exhaustion, their yearning for grander things. And it's no wonder. Russell Crowe, Minnie Driver, Robin Williams, Kevin Bacon, Queen Latifah, Andie MacDowell, Julianne Moore, Debra Winger, James Gandolfini, Geena Davis, Marcia Gay Harden, Madonna, Jessica Lange, Steve Buscemi, Al Pacino, Bette Midler, Sandra Bullock and Gwyneth Paltrow are but a few who have done time as real life waiters, busboys, bartenders, or hosts. And yet sadly, with all this experience to utilize, most restaurant films come across as stilted, inauthentic, and boring.

Alice's Restaurant

(US 1969)

Directed by Irving Penn. With Arlo Guthrie, James Broderick, Pat Quinn, Tina Chen

Singer Arlo Guthrie stars in this film based on his popular song of the same name. The movie itself was not a hit, perhaps because of its jaded take on counterculture idealism. Today, Arlo's sweet tempered, garbage dumping hippie hero looks more like a callous environmental villain. Still, the film is a bittersweet evocation of the home front during the Vietnam War, when a boy could get into trouble just for wearing his hair long and young Americans were yearning for a sense of community that their suburban upbringings had failed to provide.

This film would be fun to see for anyone who lived in the Sixties or a younger person who wants to see a realistic film with the true attitudes and experiences of the era.

The Alice's restaurant of the film is a working class New England diner where the words health food or organic would leave the customers and probably Alice herself blank faced. The menu is all over the map with Italian, Polish, and American fare taking equal billing.

For my menu I've chosen some simple recipes from the era that are more California influenced than those of Alice.

Earth Mother Oatmeal Bread
Hippy Lentil Soup
Kitchen Sink Salad
Marijuana Brownies

Earth Mother Oatmeal Bread

½ cup butter
¼ cup honey or molasses
1 t salt
One package yeast
Several cups of flour
1 cup of non-instant oatmeal
2 cups of boiling water

1. Preheat the oven to 325.
2. Place the oatmeal in the hot water adding the salt, molasses, and butter.
3. Blend.
4. Dissolve the yeast in water warm with a pinch of sugar.
5. When the oat mixture has cooled to hand temperature, add the yeast.
6. Add enough flour to form a soft dough.
7. Let rise, covered, until doubled in bulk.
8. Punch down and form into two loaves.
9. Place in buttered bread pans and cover, letting rise until the loaves just reach the top of the pan.
10. Bake for about fifty minutes to an hour.
11. Serve hot, slathered with butter.

Hippy Lentil Soup

1¼ cup lentils
1½ cups canned whole tomatoes
1 medium onion, chopped
4 medium garlic cloves, chopped
4 scallions, chopped
½ cup fresh Italian parsley, chopped
1 T turmeric
1 t ground ginger
1 T paprika
Salt, pepper, and a pinch of cayenne

1. Rinse and drain the lentils.
2. Place them in a large pot.
3. Add five cups of water and all the other ingredients.
4. Bring to a boil.
5. Then reduce heat and simmer gently for about one hour until thick.
6. Remove then process in a food processor for thirty seconds.
7. Return to pot, reheat and adjust seasonings.

Kitchen Sink Salad

It was popular to throw everything possible into a salad in the 60s and early 70s. You don't have to add the kitchen sink but throw in cucs, tomatoes, grated carrots, grated cheese, sliced radishes, sprouts, and some sunflowers seeds.

For an authentic feel eat this meal with a jug of Almaden Red Wine.

Marijuana Brownies

8 oz. chopped bittersweet chocolate
6 T butter
¼ t salt
½ t vanilla
1 cup sugar
2 eggs
¼ cup flour
1 cup walnuts

1. Makes 12.
2. Preheat oven to 325.
3. Melt the butter and the chocolate n the top of a double boiler or bain-marie.
4. Remove from the heat and add the salt, vanilla, and sugar.
5. Whisk in he eggs, one at a time.
6. Add the flour and mix until smooth.
7. Add the nuts.
8. Bake in a buttered 8 inch square pan for 35 to 40 minutes
9. Do not overbake.
10. If you decide to use an "extra" ingredient infuse the marijuana in the melted butter, then drain using the butter instead of the green matter in the recipe.

Big Night
(US 1996)

Directed by Campbell Scott and Stanley Tucci with Stanley Tucci, Ian Holm, Minnie Driver, Isabella Rossellini

"To eat good food is to be close to God."

It's mambo time as two 1950's New Jersey brothers struggle to make a success of their Italian restaurant without compromising their culinary standards. They wind up staking everything on an impending visit by celebrity singer Louis Prima. Tensions rise, bonds are tested, and the sheer joy of cooking wafts off the screen like a scintillating kitchen aroma. Anyone who has worked at or eaten at a restaurant could enjoy this film. I don't love it as much as most food lovers, but I can recommend it anyway.

The Movie Menu

Risotto with Shrimp and Scallops with a side of Spaghetti and Meatballs

(The unsophisticated customers insist on their old standby spag and balls rejecting more delicate delights such as risotto.)

Antipasti
Foccaccia
Crostini with Goat cheese
Risotto Tricolore
Timpano
Roast Chicken
Roast pig
Spinach
Asparagus
Artichokes
Whole Fish
Fruit
Nuts
Amoretti

For your own big night tell your guests to wear their snazziest suits with thin ties or prettiest vintage 1950's dresses. Play Louis Prima's Greatest Hits; Say it With a Slap, or Wild, Cool and Swinging. For dancing play Mambo, Mambo; Mambo Swing; or Mambo Fever one and two.

I've lightened up the feast so you'll still be able to walk or mambo after dining from this menu.

Frascati
Antipasti
Focaccia

Risotto Tricolore
Orvieto, Pinot Grigio, or Soave

Timpano
Valpolicella or Chianti Classico

Salad

Zuppa Inglese
Amoretti

Frangelico, Galliano, Sambuca, or Amoretto
Espresso

Antipasti

Salami or sausages, Prosciutto, pepperoni, marinated artichoke hearts, marinated asparagus spears, olives, capers, tomatoes, bite sized celery sticks, and sliced fennel, are all traditional antipasti. You can buy them from your local Italian deli or purchase packaged meats such as Columbus or Gallo brand from a grocery store. From a jar, Mezzetta Brands offer baby corn, Brussels sprouts, baby carrots, or giardiniera, which is a complete pre-marinated antipasti. Serve with breadsticks such as Musso or Italbrand or fresh, frozen, or packaged foccaccia.

Risotto Tricolore

Use the recipe for risotto recipe from Dinner with Friends omitting the squash or pumpkin.

Prepared pesto sauce

Prepared marina sauce
Grated Parmesan
2 T butter

1. Just before the rice is tender (about 20 minutes) remove from heat.
2. Divide the risotto into three parts.
3. Add prepared pesto sauce to one part, prepared marina sauce to the second part and add grated Parmesan and the butter to the third portion.
4. Place each portion on a platter (a rectangular is ideal) with the three colors touching, but not blending. The result represents the three colors of the Italian flag.

Timpano

Quite a fuss is made over this homey dish on the Big Night.

Two sheets prepared frozen pastry crust, thawed
One package mozzarella, sliced or grated
One package penne rigate
Prepared meatballs (recipe follows)
2 hard boiled eggs, coarsely chopped
Mammarella or Newman's Own pasta sauce

1. Line a spring form pan with one sheet of dough.
2. Prebake for 15 minutes at 350.
3. Cool.
4. Boil the pasta according to instructions.
5. Rinse and place aside.
6. Fry the meatballs.

1 pound ground beef
1 cup homemade or prepared breadcrumbs
1 egg
½ cup chopped parsley

½ cup Parmesan
One chopped onion
3 cloves chopped garlic
Salt and pepper
Olive oil for frying

1. Mix all the ingredients.
2. Form balls about ½ inches in diameter.
3. Heat olive oil and brown balls all around until crisp.
4. To assemble the timpano:
5. Beat the white of an egg.
6. Roll out the second crust.
7. Pour the cooked pasta, the sauce, the mozzarella, the eggs and the meatballs into the spring form and crust.
8. Cover with the unbaked crust.
9. Brush the top crust with egg white and pierce with a fork to make several small steam holes.
10. Bake 45 to 50 minutes at 350.
11. Serve hot.

Salad

Any fresh crisp salad greens will do. Toss with Italian dressing such as Bernstein's or Cardini's. For authenticity place good virgin olive oil and tart red wine vinegar, coarse salt and fresh ground pepper, on the table and let the guests dress their own salad.

Italian Dessert

Although the diners in Big Night haven't any room for this dessert, since I lightened the menu I thought you could handle this old-fashioned favorite.

Zuppa Inglese (English Soup)

Premade sponge cake, angel cake, or pound cake, cut into three parts
1 cup berry jam
1 cup rum
Custard (recipe follows)
Whipped cream
Fresh, frozen, or glanced fruit or fruitlings (optional)

1. In a pretty serving dish place, one third of the cake.
2. Spread with ⅓ cup jam.
3. Dampen with ⅓ cup of rum.
4. Pour in ⅓ of the custard.
5. Repeat the process until all the ingredients are used.
6. Let sit in the fridge for at least two hours before serving.
7. Decorate with fruit.

Custard

3 eggs
4 egg yolks
⅓ cup sugar
3 ½ cups whole milk, scalded
1 t vanilla

1. In a double boiler blend the eggs and yolks.
2. Stir in sugar, then milk.
3. Stir over low heat for around 8 minutes until the custard coats the back of a spoon.
4. Remove from heat.
5. Stir in vanilla.
6. Chill.

Now serve coffee, cigars, and Italian liqueurs.

Dinner Rush

(US 2001)

Directed by Bob Giraldi with Danny Aiello, Eduardo Ballerini, Kirk Acevedo, Sandra Bernhard.

A low-key family run Italian -American restaurant, with a lingering scent of the mob, is taken over by the celebrity chef son.

The hot young chef's signature dish is this and it's pretty damn delicious yet simple enough for even mere film lovers to make.

Lobster Pasta in Champagne Cream

4 T butter
2 10 to 12 oz. lobster tails, thawed if frozen
6 green onions, sliced
½ cup basil
1 ⅓ cup whipping cream
1 -8 oz. bottle of clam juice
1 cup Champagne
12 oz. of fettuccini
¼ cup Parmesan cheese

1. Melt butter.
2. Add lobster tails and cook until bright red, about five minutes.
3. Cover and cook another 6 minute.
4. Remove.
5. Take off shell and cut meat into ½ inch pieces.
6. Or you can use leftover lobster. If there is such a thing.
7. Add basil and mushrooms to the skillet.
8. Sauté until softened.
9. Add the champagne to taste and clam juice and reduce until half volume.
10. Meanwhile boil pasta.
11. Drain.
12. Add the cream to the reduced clam juice mixture.

13. Boil until thickened.
14. Reduce heat to low.
15. Add lobster
16. Heat through quickly.
17. Season to taste.
18. Pour sauce over pasta.
19. Add cheese.
20. Italians don't use Parmesan with seafood. Italian Americans do.
21. Toss and serve.

No Reservations

(US 2007)

The American remake was directed by Scott Hicks starring Catherine Zeta-Jones with Aaron Eckhart and Patricia Clarkson. The signature dishes were quail and truffle ravioli.

Mostly Martha

(Germany 2002)

Directed by Sandra Nettelback with Martina Gedeck, Sergio Castellitto, and Maxime Foerst. St. Martha is the patron saint of chefs.

Mostly Martha shows the imperfect life of a perfectionist chef caught up in the food frenzy of the 1990's Her obsessed and unpeopled life changes after she inherits her young niece and befriends a stereotypically life loving Italian. Soup Nazi meets Roberto Begnini. No nothing could be that bad. Why, Martha even learns to eat antipasti while seated on the floor! Clichéd, but interesting food scenes showcase Martha's underwhelming specialties. And I've made them so simple you don't have to be a tight ass chef to prepare them.

Italian antipasti (See *Big Night*)
Salmon in Basil Sauce

Salmon in Basil Sauce

4 salmon steaks
1 bottle of clam juice or one part water to one part white wine
1 cube of butter
4 T chopped basil
2 t lemon juice

1. Poach the fish in simmering liquid to cover for 8 minutes per inch of thickness.
2. Beat the butter with basil and lemon juice.
3. Serve over hot fish.

Martha's signature desert is crème brulèe. Which is pretty standard fare. Because it is best made with crème Brule dishes and a torch or salamander I'll suggest you eat another desert such as Floating Island when celebrating Martha.

Waitress

(US 2007)

Directed and written by Adrienne Shelly with Keri Russell, Cheryl Hines, and Andy Griffith. Shelly was murdered before the film came out.

A hapless young woman married to a brute finds an outlet and eventually a better life through baking pies at a diner. Her imaginatively named desserts include Baby Screamin' It's Head Off In the Middle of the Night and Ruinin' My Life Pie, and more simply Mermaid Pie, which I have recreated here. This pie would be fun for kids to make and frankly I think they may be the only ones who'd want to eat it.

Mermaid Pie

1 cup graham cracker crumbs
½ cup flaked sweet coconut
5 t butter
34 large marshmallows
½ cup whole milk
1½ cups heavy whipping cream
Sugar to taste
Blue, and or green, food coloring

1. Combine butter, crumbs and coconut. Press into a nine-inch pie tin.
2. Bake for ten minutes.
3. Cool.
4. Melt the marshmallows with the milk in a double boiler.
5. Add blue or green food coloring to your preference.
6. Whip the cream and add sugar to taste. Add whichever color you did not add to the filling.
7. Pour filling into piecrust.
8. Cover with whipped cream.

Restaurant Film Trivia Quiz

You'll work up an appetite trying to recall all the films involving comical cooks, shady chefs, rivaling restaurateurs, funny food writers, caterers, or cooking schools. Several films simply depict the touching struggle to make a go of an eatery.

While dinner is cooking, name as many such films as you can. Try to remember all the French, Chinese, and horror films that depict restaurants as well. The winner gets dinner out of course!

While you're at it, which movie stars own or have owned restaurants?

CHAPTER SIX

Tea and Sympathy (US 1956)

Afternoon Teas and Desserts

A wonderful way to share a wintry afternoon with friends is to host a matinee tea. Bake some shortbread, fix a few finger sandwiches, and brew a pot of Ceylon, then sit back and switch on the DVD.

I've selected costume dramas and period pieces, which include such ladylike themes as the servant problem, cases of mistaken identity, religious and racial intolerance, adultery, illegitimacy, hidden homosexuality, divorce, totalitarianism, and murder.

The Governess

(UK 1998)

Directed by Sandra Goldbacher with Minnie Driver, Tom Wilkinson, and Harriet Walker

Minnie Driver plays a mid-Victorian Jewess from a well-off family. Following her father's death she is forced by her family's reduced circumstances to pass herself off as a Gentile to obtain work as a governess. The independent girl becomes involved with her employer's passion… photography… and passionately involved with her employer as well. The girl is not very impressed with the food she eats at her employer's home and craves the honey cake she used to enjoy at home.

Jewish Honey Cake

2 ½ cups flour
2 t baking powder
2 t cinnamon
½ t baking soda
½ t salt
½ ground cloves
3 eggs
I cup honey
1 cup sugar
1 cup oil
½ cup prepared coffee
¼ cup water

1. Heat oven to 350.
2. Butter a Bundt pan.
3. Sift dry ingredients.
4. Beat the eggs then add to the dries.
5. Then add the other fluids and mix until blended.
6. Pour batter into pan and bake for 50 minutes until a toothpick comes out clean.
7. Serve with strong coffee or tea.

The Importance of Being Ernest

A classic Victorian comedy of manners and false identity from the play by Oscar Wilde.
(UK 1952)

Anthony Asquith directed Dame Edith Evans, Ralph Richardson and Michael Redgrave in this great version.
(UK2002)

Oliver Parker directed Rupert Everett, Colin Firth and Reece Witherspoon in a second rate version.

Gosford Park

(US 2001)

Drama, Comedy Mystery

Directed by Robert Altman with Maggie Smith, Jeremy Northam, Kristin Scott Thomas, Clive Owen, Alan Bates, Helen Mirrin, Emily Watson, et al

Set at an English country house shooting party in 1932, murder, adultery, mistaken and false identity, incessant snobbery, thwarted romance, and a matinee idol combine to make great, good fun.

A Simple Homey Tea

Buy packaged English muffins, crumpets, or scones. Use your favorite jam or something a little unusual such as rose petal jelly, elderberry, or gooseberry jam. Buy some clotted cream or whip up some heavy whipped cream. Get your favorite packaged but delicate cookies such as Pepperidge Farm. Purchase thin sandwich bread such as Orowheat, cut off the crusts and spread thinly with butter. Even plain bread and butter are delicious with some milky tea. To create some basic tea sandwiches, peel an English cucumber and slice into rounds. Spread the sandwich bread with softened cream cheese and place the cucumbers on the bread. Sprinkle lightly with salt, pepper, and dill. Cover with a second slice of bread. Cut into thirds. Brew a pot of English or Irish breakfast tea and serve in cups, not mugs, with milk, honey, and lemon slices. Bring out your prettiest plates and cups, a lacey or floral tablecloth, and set out real napkins. Place an old-fashioned bouquet in the middle of the tea table and enjoy.

A Fancy Tea Party

To stage a glamorous tea party procure the Gosford Park soundtrack or CD's of early Bing Crosby, Noel Coward, or Gershwin tunes. Guests can wear elegant tea length dresses with long pearls, gloves, hats, crisp suits, or jodhpurs and riding gear, or anything tweedy. The men can wear nice suits or tweedy professorial attire.

"If her own mother had a heart attack she'd think it's less important than one of Lady Sylvia's farts," says Emily Lloyd's character of the Housekeeper, played by Helen Mirrin.

The Menu

Scones, Cream and Jam
Watercress Sandwiches
Victoria Sandwich Cake
Welsh Rarebit Savories
Stilton, Cheddar, or Huntsman Cheeses
Salmon Mousse
Bread and Butter
Earl Grey or Black Currant Tea
Martinis (See Snack and Drink)
Bloody Marys
Tea and Champagne Cocktail
Sidecars (See Snack and Drink)

Scones and Clotted Cream

Makes 8
2 cups flour
¼ cup sugar
3 t baking powder
One stick butter
½ cup currents
1 egg
½ cup milk, blended with egg

Zest of one orange or lemon

1. Place flour, powder, zest, and sugar in a food processor or bowl.
2. Add the butter and blend.
3. Add the egg and milk and blend.
4. Add the currents and blend.
5. Roll out and cut into rounds or place in a round baking pan and score.
6. Bake until golden for 25 minutes.

Serve with a bowl of clotted cream and a bowl of jam.

Watercress Sandwiches

Watercress
Cream cheese
Salt and pepper
Thin brown or white sandwich bread with the crust removed

1. Pluck leaves off the watercress
2. Add to the cream cheese and blend with salt and pepper to taste.
3. Spread on bread.
4. Cover with second slice of bread.
5. Cut into triangles or three "fingers "

Victoria Sandwich Cake

This classic cake is a teatime standard.
8 oz. flour
8 oz. sugar
8 oz. butter
4 eggs
3 t baking powder
Vanilla extract
Pinch of salt

A dribble of milk
Raspberry jam
Whipped Cream
Strawberries

1. Preheat the oven to 350.
2. Beat the eggs and sugar until smooth and fluffy and the sugar is dissolved.
3. Add the eggs one at a time blending after each addition.
4. Sift the flour, salt, and baking powder.
5. Add to the batter.
6. Bake in two greased and floured 8 inch cake tins for 25 to 30 minutes.
7. Cool and remove.
8. On one layer spread raspberry jam and whipped cream or if it is spring or summer fresh cut strawberries.

Welsh Rarebit Savouries

For 8
4 t milk or beer or stout
4 t Worcestershire sauce
2 oz. butter
2 t dry English mustard
½ t salt
½ t pepper
12 oz grated sharp cheddar cheese
8 slices of white bread, grilled until golden on one side or toasted

1. Combine everything but the cheese and bread in a saucepan.
2. Heat then add cheese until melted.
3. Spread on bread on the white side or either side if toasted
4. Grill 2 to 3 minutes until bubbly.
5. Then cut into triangles as finger food.

Tea and Champagne Cocktail

2 cups strong made tea, cold
1 bottle champagne
1 T Cointreau per glass
Zest of orange for garnish
One sugar cube per glass

1. Put sugar, Cointreau, and zest into champagne glasses.
2. Pour in tea and champers

Far From Heaven

(US 2000)

Directed by Todd Haynes with Julianne Moore, Dennis Quaid, and Dennis Haysbert, this homage to the euphemistic melodramas of the 1950's is shot in New England autumnal colors instead of black and white. It explores homosexuality and race relations through the life of a Connecticut housewife with robotic children. Julianne Moore, as the wife, and her women friends get together to eat cake and down a pitcher of daiquiris. I've combined the two in one easy to make recipe using cake mixes, which were just coming onto the scene in the 1950's.

Daiquiri Cake

1 package of lemon cake mix
1 package of vanilla instant pudding
4 eggs
½ cup oil
1 heaping t lime zest
½ cup sour drink mix

1. Mix and beat for thirty seconds on medium speed or two minutes by hand.
2. Pour into a greased and floured Bundt pan.
3. Bake forty-five minutes at 350 until toothpick comes out clean.
4. Cool and glaze.

Glaze

One cup powdered sugar
1 t lime zest
2 T lime juice or lime and sour mix or daiquiri

Daiquiris

2 oz. rum
2 oz. lime juice
½ t sugar
Ice

The Joy Luck Club
(US 1993)

Directed by Wayne Wang with France Nuyen, Kieu Chinh, Tsui Chin, and Lisa Lu

A San Franciscan seeks to understand her difficult relationship with her mother by uncovering the mother's tragic past in her native China. In doing so she learns about the histories of her mother's three best friends who also have quite some stories to tell.

The mother creates a special crab dish, but you won' be able to make "best quality" crab like she does. Order out from your favorite Chinese restaurant then serve this gooey confection, their family favorite.

Chocolate Peanut Butter Pie

One prepared crust, baked at 400 for fifteen minutes until golden brown and cooled

Four egg yolks, whisked in a bowl
⅔ cup sugar
3½ T cornstarch
1 T butter

1 t vanilla extract
1 cup semisweet chocolate chips
1 cup peanut butter

1. Combine sugar and cornstarch in a medium sized saucepan.
2. Whisk in half and half.
3. Bring to a boil whisking steadily.
4. Boil for one minute. Remove from heat.
5. Pour half of mixture while whisking, into yolks.
6. Return yolk mixture to heat.
7. Add butter and vanilla.
8. Place chips and peanut butter in a bowl
9. Add the hot custard mixture and stir until smooth.
10. Pour into piecrust evenly.
11. Cool for one hour.
12. Refrigerate for at least two hours.
13. Cover with plastic to prevent crust from forming.

The Prime of Miss Jean Brodie

(UK 1969)

Ronald Neame directed Maggie Smith, Pamela Franklin, and Gordon Jackson in this film version of Muriel Spark's novel.

Miss Brodie, that fascinating fascist, is a fine cook who creates charlotte Russe, sweetbreads à la Milanese, and lasagna verde for her favorite girrrls. Such dishes must have been a delight to the palate, but possibly an assault to the digestion of young Depression era Scottish girls. Those dishes do not exist in the novel, but are an addition from the screenwriter. It's an amusing character enhancement because Miss Brodie chooses her menu from countries lead by dictators.

I won't have you slaving away to satisfy the likes of Jean Brodie. Nothing would suit this film better than a nice scotch shortbread taken with strong Scottish breakfast tea, a dram of whiskey, or a dribble of Drambuie.

Pitcaithly Shortbread

Preheat oven to 325
2 oz. blanched almonds, chopped
6 oz. flour
2 oz. sugar
4 oz. butter
1 ounce orange, lemon or lime zest or any combination thereof

1. Rub the flour butter and sugar together until it resembles breadcrumbs.
2. Add the peel and almonds and mix.
3. Push into a round pie tin or cake tin.
4. Bake in the oven for 30 minutes until golden brown.
5. Cool for ten minutes then slice into 8 wedges.
6. Cool completely before removing from pan.

The Group

(US 1966)

Directed by Sydney Lumet with Candice Bergen, Shirley Knight, Carrie Nye

The Group is the story of eight Vassar graduates leading their post college lives from the depression until WWII. The bipolar father of one of the girls loves to cook when he's manic. He whips up everything from chili to duck à l'orange. But for the most part, the characters are living within limited means and with minimal cooking skills. At the wedding of one girl they feast on Baked Alaska, which was popular in the 1930's when the book takes place, and was on restaurant menus when the movie was filmed in the 1960's. This recipe is an adaptation from the Brown Derby Restaurant in Los Angeles, a favorite eatery of the stars during the glamour era of Hollywood.

Brown Derby Baked Alaska

⅓ cup sifted cake flour
¼ t salt
½ t baking powder
1 large egg yolk
⅓ cup sugar
½ t grated orange rind
4 t boiling water
2 t orange juice
½ t vanilla extract
2 egg whites

1. Beat yolks.
2. Add sugar and rind.
3. Add water and beat for one minute.
4. Add juice and vanilla.
5. Add dry ingredients and beat until just mixed.
6. Beat whites until frothy.
7. Add cream of tartar and beat until they are stiff but not dry.
8. Fold the whites into the batter.
9. Pour into a buttered and floured cake pan.
10. Bake 15 to 20 minutes or until a toothpick inserted in the middle comes out clean.
11. Cool upside down, and then remove from pan.

Meringue

8 room temperature egg whites
1/8 t salt
2 cups sugar
2 t vanilla
2 t or more of orange liqueur.

1. Preheat oven to 500.
2. Beat whites until frothy.
3. Add the cream of tartar.

4. Add the sugar steadily while whipping until whites are stiff but not dry.
5. Add vanilla.
6. Place the cake on a baking sheet.
7. Drizzle with liqueur.
8. Place ice cream on top of the cake.
9. Frost the cake with the meringue thoroughly making sure the ice cream is covered.
10. But don't make the meringue too thick or it won't cook through.
11. Bake 3 to 5 minutes.

Fried Green Tomatoes

(US 1991)

Jon Avnet directed Kathy Bates and Jessica Tandy

An overall likable film with some bland and weak points sauced over with some memorable characters and scenes about female friendships. Because there is a cookbook called The Original Whistle Stop Café Cookbook," I won't repeat those recipes here. So get your best girlfriends together and serve some blueberry pie. Give individual pots of honey as favors.

Not-So-Famous Movie Quotes Trivia Quiz

Directors, actors, and characters in films have some great lines about food. Who said these?

1. Which director, whose titles sometimes are food titles said this, "Why does man kill? He kills for food. And not only food: frequently there must be a beverage."

2. What famous director, who may well have made a morose dinner guest said this, "Conversation is the enemy of good food and wine."

3. A director whose religion may have precluded him from eating mollusks anyway. "I will not eat oysters. I want my food dead—not sick, not wounded, dead."

4. What bewitching early cinema star said this? "Age is something that doesn't matter, unless you are cheese."

5. What famous funnyman from a trio said?" Time flies like an arrow. Fruit flies like a banana."

6. What ultra famous Babe from Brooklyn said this:" Success to me is having ten honeydew melons and eating the top off of each one."

7. The dying process begins the minute we are born, but it accelerates during dinner parties.

8. "Do you know why we clink glasses before we drink? It's so that all the senses are involved. We touch the glass. We smell the drink. We see its color. We taste it. Hearing is the only sense that doesn't participate unless we create a sound..."

Fabulous Food Scenes Trivia Quiz

In the movies, food often doesn't actually wind up in the characters mouths. Toast takes off as though launched from Cape Canaveral or mistossed flapjacks glue themselves to the ceiling only to succumb to gravity when a character's head is underneath.

Name your favorite off beat food scenes or use the following hints. The winner gets a pot of cactus jelly or root beer jelly beans...or anything edible but not all that appetizing.

1. A woman's corpse is hidden in a truckload of potatoes.

2. A Breugelesque ranch barbecue is the best scene in this dreadful movie.

3. Castaways cook a giant crab by flipping it into a geyser.

4. Jack Lemmon strains spaghetti on a tennis racket.

5. A prisoner of War in WWII France waxes so poetically about pommes frites you can taste them.

6. Three gorgeous women, believing that life is just a bowl of cherries, pop Bings into their mouths not knowing the disastrous effect such an innocent gesture will have.

7. Is it an act of liberation when the nanny burns her bra or just an accident while stirring the pot?

8. "Cooking is cruel. These carrots have been murdered," proclaims a British fruitarian to her host Hugh Grant.

9. Elizabeth Taylor faints after viewing a calf's head on the table at a Texan Barbecue.

10. Buttering someone up takes on a whole new meaning in this famous 70's film.

11. It's meals on wheels when Lucy prepares dinner while Desi does the driving

12. Eddie serves himself up as the main course at a campy castle.

13. A couple attempts to cook shellfish.

14. Would you eat blindfolded from your fridge?

15. A Mutt and a miss mutt enjoy pasta together.

16. A guest at a Jewish wedding hacks the head off the chopped chicken liver.

17. A peevish Meg Ryan scolds Tom Hanks for eating the garnish off a party platter.

18. Richard Dreyfus builds a mountain of mash.

19. Peculiar potions and curious cakes make Alice taller or smaller.

20. A pastry maker's offerings change the attitudes of a straitlaced French town.

21. A Mexican girl, whose mother has thwarted her love life, uses food as revenge for those who have wronged her

22. A Brazilian chef tries to win back her boyfriend through food.

23. Eating a doctored apple causes a young girl to become a live-in caregiver for seven stature challenged men.

24. A peckish belle stuffs a dirty tuber into her mouth.

25. A 20's era man discusses the fig in relation to female anatomy.

26. An unusual oyster eating method.

27. A woman doesn't use her hands to prepare food.

28. Scantily clad slave girls crush hardboiled eggs between their two stomachs and slice the resultant scantily clad egg through a lyre in this musical update of the ancient Roman comedies.

29. The search for the perfect egg salad recipe motivates this spy spoof.

30. No one waffles about his or her feeling for this famous breakfast scene.

31. A pudgy, barely competent, chain smoking, Londoner accidentally creates blue soup for her dinner guests.

32. A misbehaving pressure cooker full of rice saves the leading man from a dinner of chicken with saffron chocolate sauce.

CHAPTER SEVEN

The Children's Hour (UK 1965)

Treats To Make with Kids

Watching a video, then recreating a dish from a film, can be a family project for a rainy afternoon or a fun idea for a slumber party.

The Little Princess
(US 1939)

Walter Lang directed Shirley Temple, Richard Green, and Anita Louise from the novel by Frances Hodgson Burnett.

A Little Princess
(US 1995)

Alfonso Cuaron, directed Eleanor Bron (who you may remember as Hermione in "Women in Love" or as the object of Dudley Moore's passion in the first brilliant "Bedazzled"), Liam Cunningham, and Liesel Matthews.

A well-off little girl attending a posh boarding school is reduced to penury when her father is killed. She is forced to become a servant where once she was a pampered student. Her loss is tempered somewhat when she befriends the Indian servant of the next-door neighbor and Becky, another servant at the school. The earlier film takes place in London where Becky is a Cockney child. The later version is set in New York City and Becky is now a little black girl.

As magical as the sudden appearance of a hot breakfast seemed to the poor and hungry girls in both versions of this film, it's a spell easily cast by any parent who wants to charm a child. As an American child, I had no idea what the kippers were which the girls so eagerly eat in the 1939 film. The 1990's version provides an equally magical breakfast, one familiar to most American children without any smoked fish to make American kids turn up their noses.

It's a lovely idea to give your little princess or prince a delicious breakfast surprise in their bedroom. You may not be able to provide the glowing coal fire that warmed Shirley Temple, but you can place a vase of sunflowers by the bed and then present your child an inexpensive East Indian trinket. As Becky in the American version wants to eat "every kind of muffin God ever made", include an array such as oatmeal, date, corn, blueberry, or our lemon muffins on your child's breakfast tray.

Tea or Hot Cocoa (See Vatel)
Orange Juice
Lemon Cinnamon Tea Muffins
Chicken Apple Sausages

Lemon Cinnamon Tea Muffins

1 cup flour
¼ t salt
1 t baking powder
½ cup butter
½ cup sugar
2 additional T sugar
3 T lemon juice
2 eggs, separated
1 t lemon peel
½ t cinnamon

1. Prepare a muffin tin by greasing and flouring enough for 18 muffins or use18 paper muffin cups.
2. Sift the flour, powder, and salt into a mixing bowl.
3. Cream the butter with the sugar until fluffy.
4. Beat the yolks lightly and add to the butter.
5. Add the lemon juice and peel, and then blend.
6. Add the flour and blend.
7. Whip the egg whites until stiff.
8. Fold the mixtures together.
9. Combine the remaining sugar and cinnamon.
10. Pour the muffins mix into tins, filling halfway full.
11. Sprinkle with the sugar mixture.
12. Bake for 1520 minutes.
13. Cool, and then remove from tins.

Willie Wonka and the Chocolate Factory

(US 1971)

Directed by Mel Stuart with Gene Wilder and Jack Albertson, from the novel Charlie and the Chocolate Factory by Roald Dahl. The author was married to actress Patricia Neal and his daughter and granddaughter Tessa and Sophie also acted in films.

This is a really weird, not altogether pleasant movie that features "The Candy Man", an oddly creepy song.

(UK 2005)

Tim Burton directs his inamorata Helena Bonham Carter and Johnny Depp, who seems destined to star in movies about chocolate.

The sweet edible possibilities from Willie Wonka and the Chocolate Factory are endless. So to simplify, I offer kid pleasing chocolate leaves and a simple chocolate sorbet that doesn't even require an ice cream freezer.

Chocolate Sorbet

2 cups water
¼ cup sugar
10 T unsweetened cocoa powder
4 oz chopped sweetened chocolate
4 T honey

1. Bring the water and sugar to a boil in a medium sized saucepan.
2. Add the cocoa powder and blend.
3. Add the chocolate and the honey and whisk smooth.
4. Let cool to room temperature then place in refrigerator to further cool
5. Process in your ice cream maker according to instructions or place in a metal bowl or ice cube trays and stir with a metal spoon every half hour or so until the sorbet forms.

Chocolate Leaves

This is a project kids love.
You will need:
Leaves
A good milk or semisweet chocolate
A baking sheet
Waxed paper
One or more pastry brushes

1. Find some smooth firm leaves like lemon, rhododendron, or camellia. Do not use eucalyptus, geraniums, ferns or any fuzzy or delicate leaf because the chocolate will not peel off properly.
2. Temper some good chocolate according to package instructions.
3. Make room in the fridge for a baking sheet covered with waxed or parchment paper.
4. With a pastry brush paint the melted chocolate on the smoothest side of the leaves and place the coated leaves on the baking tray.

5. Cool in the fridge until the chocolate is completely firm.
6. Peel the leaves off the chocolate and discard them.
7. Enjoy the chocolate leaves as candy or use them to garnish the chocolate sorbet.

James and the Giant Peach

(UK 1996

Henry Selick directed Pete Postlewaite and the voices of Joanna Lumley, Jane Leeves, and Susan Sarandon from the novel by Roald Dahl.

A rampaging rhino orphans a happy English lad. Forced to live with two unpleasant aunts, his relief comes in the form of a spider that helps him plans his escape to New York City.

Peach Ice Cream

2 cups ripe peaches, pitted and chopped
½ cup sugar
¼ cup light corn syrup
1 ½ cups half and half
1 cup heavy cream
4 egg yolks
1 t lemon juice
½ t vanilla extract
½ t almond extract (optional)

1. Combine the peaches, ¼ cup sugar, and corn syrup in a saucepan over medium heat.
2. Heat for about five minutes.
3. Set aside.
4. Combine the half and half, the ½ cup cream and bring to a simmer.
5. Whisk the egg yolks and sugar together.
6. Pour hot cream into the yolk mixture, stirring.
7. Return to the saucepan and heat gently stirring with a wooden spoon about six minutes or until a custard forms.

8. Add the peaches and the custard to a food processor or food mill and puree until smooth.
9. Add vanilla and cream.
10. If the peaches are not ultra ripe, adding a dash of almond extract may help bring out their flavor.
11. Cool in the fridge for at least an hour until cold.
12. Pour into ice cream freezer and proceed according to manufacturer's instructions.

Peach Melba was named after the Australian opera singer Nellie Melba. Melba toast also bears her name. Taste this simple but wonderfully summery dessert. Then try a piece of dry Melba toast. See which you prefer.

1. Scoop a small serving of peach ice cream into a dish.
2. Place one half of a ripe, juicy peach over the ice cream.
3. Pour some raspberry puree over this.

To make raspberry puree, simply food process some fresh or frozen raspberries and add sugar to taste. You can force the puree through a sieve with the back of a large spoon if you don't want the seeds.

The Lion, the Witch and the Wardrobe

(US 1979)

Animated by Bill Melender from the children's book series by C.S. Lewis.

(UK 2006) Directed by Adam Adamson with Tilda Swinton as the Witch.

Four WW 2 era London children, evacuated to their uncle's countryside home, find an amazing wardrobe through which they gain entry to the snowy world of Narnia. The kids are offered Turkish delight candy, which unlike its innocuous Middle Eastern counterpart has addictive charms.

Most American children have never experienced Turkish delight and want to give it a try after seeing this film. You can find authentic forms at Middle Eastern shops or, using our recipe, you can make a version of delight that can be creative in its flavoring, coloring, and additions.

Turkish Delight

One cup orange juice
One cup water
Juice of one large lemon
6 envelopes of gelatin
2 cups sugar
1 T lemon rind
1 T orange rind
Powdered sugar
½ cup slightly chopped pistachios, hazelnuts, or walnuts (optional)
Food coloring (optional)
1 T of orange flower water (optional)

1. Heat the liquids in a nonmetallic saucepan.
2. Dissolve the gelatin, packet by packet, into the mixture and cook for four minutes over medium flame.
3. Add the sugar and citrus rind.
4. Bring to a boil and then simmer, stirring once in a while, for fifteen to twenty minutes.
5. Add the nutmeats, coloring, or flower water if desired.
6. Pour into a 9x9 baking pan to cool.
7. When solid, cut into pieces and dust with powdered sugar.

Little Women

In 1933 Cukor directed Katharine Hepburn.

In 1949 Mervyn Leroy directed Elizabeth Taylor.

In 1994 Gillian Armstrong directed Winona Ryder from the novel by Louisa May Alcott.

This beloved classic depicts the Civil War era New England March family. Louisa Alcott's own life as the daughter of bohemian intellectuals who founded a Utopian community would have been much more interesting than this treacley tale of four goody goody sisters. But poverty forced Alcott to write potboilers and finally "Little Women" and " Little Men."

The March sisters make biscuits in every version of Little Women. In the book they also bake a squash pie. I've combined the squash with the biscuits using an old-fashioned New England recipe. This is one way to get the kids to eat their vegetables. These are absolutely delicious!

New England Squash Biscuits

1 package of yeast
½ cup lukewarm water
6 or more cups of flour, sifted
¾ cup sugar
½ t salt
4 T melted butter
2 eggs
1 ½ cups cooked, pureed, winter squash
1 cup scalded milk, cooled

Dissolve the yeast into the water.

1. Add one T sugar and ¼ cup flour, then cover and let sit in a warm place for 45 minutes.
2. Add one cup flour, the rest of the sugar, the butter, the salt, the eggs, and the pureed squash.

3. Add the remaining flour, alternating with the milk, beginning and ending with the flour.
4. Add enough flour to make a soft, pliable dough.
5. Cover and let rise in a warm spot for about 1½ hour or until the dough has doubled in bulk.
6. Flour a board and your hands and knead the sticky dough for about five minutes.
7. Divide the dough in half and roll out to ½ inch thickness.
8. Cut into 2 to 2½ inch rounds.
9. Preheat the oven to 425.
10. Place the biscuits on ungreased sheets and let them rise, covered for ½ hour.
11. Bake risen biscuits for fifteen minutes until the tops are browning.

Serve hot with butter or use for mini sandwiches

Fighting with Food Trivia Quiz

1. Just cause she's your best friend doesn't mean you don't want to shove blueberry pie in her face at the Whistle Stop Café.

2. Two hams duke it out with a literal ham.

3. Care for some custard pie, Ollie?

4. When does this trio not have a food fight?

5. Three sisters bicker over their dying father and then let loose in the kitchen with each other.

CHAPTER EIGHT

Home for the Holidays (US 1995)

Holiday Food, Films, and Trivia

It's customary during the holidays to gather people of varying age, interests, and inclinations under one roof to share bountiful meals and copious leisure time. While expectations of enjoyment are high, with disparate traditions, complicated family blending, and old grudges and disappointments reigniting, tensions often arise. Early films, with their heart warming Christmas Eves and Thanksgivings anyone would be thankful for, showed people an ideal. By the 1970's, filming harmonious families, grateful children, and perfectly prepared repasts had gone out of fashion. In their place came more realistic scenes about the struggles of families to put up with each other. In these pictures, sometimes the problems are solved and sometimes frictions remain insurmountable. Directors choose to depict many a familial confrontation at the Thanksgiving table, but they rarely depict a toxic Christmas.

Watching a carefully selected film together can be a great way to keep people of different generations and interests entertained. And a time to play some "food in film" trivia quizzes. For those who don't actually "go home" for the holidays, watching certain family holiday films might warm their lonesome hearts. Watching others might make them remember why they stayed away from the family get-together to begin with.

A Christmas Carol

This perennial family favorite has been filmed in the US and the UK repeatedly from 1908 until the present in cinematic, televised, and animated versions.

In 1938, Edwin Marin directed Reginald Owen, Gene Lockhart, and Leo G. Carroll in a classic version of the tale. In 2000, David Hugh Jones directed Patrick Stewart, Richard E. Grant, and Joel Grey in another excellent version. Both are available on video.

Scrooge, a grouchy old geezer, learns compassion after three ghosts scare him half to death. Following are two old-fashioned seasonal treats.

Plum Pudding
Smoking Bishop

Don't panic, you can have a plum pudding for Christmas without adding suet, searching for plums, trying to find a pudding basin, or steaming the thing for hours. This simple and satisfying baked version can be made by anyone.

Baked Plum Pudding

1 cup brown sugar
½ cup butter
6 eggs
¼ cup flour
1 t cinnamon
½ t allspice or nutmeg
A dash of clove powder
1 oz slivered almonds, pecans, walnuts or a mixture of all
1 cup golden or red raisins and / or dried currents
½ apple or pear, minced
2 cups breadcrumbs
⅓ cup candied orange peel, optional

1. Blend the butter and sugar until smooth.
2. Add one egg at a time, mixing well after each addition.

3. Add the spices to the flour.
4. Toss the nuts and fruits in the flour until coated.
5. Combine the two mixtures until fully moistened.
6. Add the breadcrumbs and if using, orange peel.
7. Pour mixture into a buttered baking dish or baking pan and bake at 375 for thirty minutes.
8. Serve with hard or soft sauce, garnished with holly.

Hard Sauce

4 oz. butter
4 oz. powdered sugar
4 T brandy or rum
Combine the ingredients.

You can leave out the "sauce" to make a soft sauce for children. Drink some spiced Christmas tea or a rich port as an accompaniment.

Smoking Bishop

4 oranges
1 grapefruit
25 whole cloves
4 oz sugar (brown or white)
1 bottle of red wine
1 bottle of port or brandy

1. Prick each fruit with five whole cloves.
2. Bake on a cookie sheet at 350 until they turn light brown.
3. Add the sugar and one bottle of red wine and the fruit to a saucepan.
4. Let sit twenty-four hours, covered. (This step is optional)
5. Add the bottle of port.
6. Heat without boiling.
7. Serve in mugs or teacups or other heatproof vessels.

Christmas in Connecticut

(US 1945)

Peter Godfrey directed Barbara Stanwyck, Sydney Greenstreet, and Reginald Gardiner

Barbara Stanwyck plays a writer who has created a fake husband, a false farm, and a fictional baby to add weight to her credibility as a food and home columnist. But she's nearly hoisted on her own knife sharpener when her publisher decides to spend Christmas with her picturesque family. In addition, as a publicity stunt, he plans on bringing along a wounded WW2 GI. Stanwyck can't even cook, so she does her best to procure a phony family and a chef to secretly prepare the meals. Naturally, mayhem ensues, but the chef cooks up some pretty good grub and so can you.

Stanwyck finds that the GI can diaper and bath a baby and can sing, dance, and play the piano as well. His character must have seemed like the ideal, both practical and entertaining, to a country full of war widows and wives separated from husbands.

The "Best Cook in America" who turns out to be the Helpless Homemaker pretends to cook up a feast of:

Salad with Cheese Dressing
Chicken Maryland
Roast Goose
Celery Soufflé
Plum Pudding (See *A Christmas Carol*)

But yes, even if you are a Helpless Homemaker you can make a similar and easy comfort meal. Without using a single ration ticket.

1940's Blue Cheese Dressing

One cup olive oil
¼ cup vinegar
½ t salt
½ t pepper
A pinch of cayenne
⅓ cup blue cheese

1. First add two T of the mixed dressing to the crumbled cheese.
2. Then blend all and serve over romaine and curly endive or your favorite greens.

Chicken Maryland

One frying chicken, cut into pieces
6 T melted butter
¼ cup flour
Salt
Pepper
A dash nutmeg
2 pieces bacon
Parsley

1. Combine the seasonings and flour.
2. Rub the chicken with melted butter, and then dredge in flour.
3. Fry bacon until brown in a skillet large enough to hold the chicken.
4. Remove.
5. Add the chicken and brown on all sides.
6. Cover and let cook for thirty minutes.
7. Add 1 cup cream.
8. Cook uncovered until cream has reduce.
9. Pour in another cup of cream.
10. Adjust for seasoning.
11. Garnish with parsley and serve with chicken gravy.

Serve with mashed or boiled potatoes.

What's Cookin?
(US 2000)

Drama Comedy

Gurinder Chada directed Joan Chen, Julianne Margulies, Mercedes Ruehl, and Alfre Woodard.

Four typical American families, living in the Fairfax district of Los Angeles, celebrate Thanksgiving in their own ways, combining their individual ethnic traditions with turkey and family trouble as trimmings. This pleasant little film depicts not only the diversity of America and American eating habits, but also the subtle differences in how people regard food for the same occasion, how they prepare it, how much effort they put into it, and which family members do the cooking.

In the immigrant Vietnamese Nguyen family only the women and girls prepare the Thanksgiving dinner. In tribute to their new American homeland, they roast a turkey, leaving half of the bird plain and half rubbed with traditional Vietnamese seasonings. The turkey burns and Kentucky Fried Chicken takes its place. The family eats spring rolls, stir-fried greens, and rice noodles using canned cranberries and canned yams to complete their American repast.

The African American couple are typical contemporary Californians. The wife expects her husband to help while she stuffs a turkey with shiitake mushrooms and oysters, steams asparagus (in November!) and grills mushrooms with red peppers. The gelatinous canned cranberry sauce is banished from this household in favor of homemade, and the highly decorative home baked pies would meet with Martha's approval. It's all to be washed down with good California red wine and champagne. But then Grandma, who hails from the South, barely knows it's Thanksgiving without her traditional mac and cheese, cornbread, and sugary fruit compote. And that's the fare that appeals most to her Angeleno grandson.

Down the street at the Avila home, all the women pitch in to make a turkey garnished by a truckload of hot peppers, with tamales, tortillas, salsa, empanadas, guacamole, and then mashed potatoes, corn on the cob, roasted yams, and fruit salad. The pies are store bought, but not the arroz con leche, a Mexican rice pudding.

The Jewish family represents midcentury American cooking where convenience is king. Every dish is scooped out of a can or store-bought. Only the older women prepare the feast: the baby boomer daughter is not allowed to lift a finger to help. The canned yams are served with red dyed maraschino cherries and marshmallows, the packaged whipped potatoes are awash in margarine, the piecrust is premade, the Jell-O mold is dressed in Cool Whip, and the dinner rolls are from a package. There are very few Americans of a certain age who will not readily recognize at least a few of the components of this meal… with or without nostalgia.

In these pages I won't tell anybody how to cook a typical Thanksgiving dinner for their family, but if you are away from home, dining alone, or putting on a pot luck for a gathering of friends, why not prepare a smattering of international foods that represent the true heart of modern America and the families in this film? And even non-cooks can prepare some of the dishes.

My Menu

Creamy Vietnamese Soup
Stuffed Turkey from "The Leopard"
Grilled Portobellos
Ginger ale Jell-O Mold
Arroz Con Leche or Creamy Orange Rice Pudding

Creamy Vietnamese Soup

3 cups chicken broth, or vegetable broth
2 standard cans coconut milk
1 whole chicken breast (optional)
⅓ pound rice vermicelli
6 T lime juice
6 T fish sauce
Chili oil to taste
Cilantro
2 garlic cloves
2 T cooking oil
4 T curry powder
2 stalks of lemongrass
10 slices of peeled ginger
1 t peppercorns
Using a saucepan sauté the garlic in the oil.

1. When you can smell the garlic add the curry powder.
2. Then pour in the coconut milk, and broth and add the lemongrass, ginger, and pepper.
3. Bring to a boil.
4. Add the chicken and poach at a simmer until cooked through, about 20 minutes.
5. Remove the chicken, cool, and shred.
6. Soak the noodles in warm water for five minutes then cook in boiling salted water for five minutes.
7. Add the chicken, broth mixture, lime juice and fish sauce. And heat through.
8. Pour into bowls over rice noodles.

Garish with chili oil and chopped cilantro if desired.

Grilled Portobellos

4 Portobello mushrooms
2 T olive oil
Salt
Pepper
Thyme
Other herbs if desired

This was my family holiday mainstay. Chock full of crunchy fruit and nuts it's about as good as jell-o can get.

Ginger Ale Salad

1 package Lime Jell-O
1 cup ginger ale
Green and red and purple grapes, halved
Red and green apples, chopped in ½ inch pieces
Chopped walnuts

1. Make the jell-o according to instructions on the package, substituting ginger ale for the cold water.
2. Place the fruit and nuts in either individual gelatin molds or a larger metal cake or pie tin.
3. Cover with the jell-o mixture and refrigerate until set.
4. Unset when ready to serve by placing molds or pan in warm water half way up the side. Unset on red lettuce leaves.

Arroz Con Leche

There are as many arroz con leche recipes as there are cooks. They are all good old rice pudding. Use the Creamy Orange Rice pudding from Chapter One. You can substitute lime or lemon for the orange and add a handful of plump raisins or some chopped nuts if that appeals.

Turkey Day Trivia Quiz

1. Four ethnically diverse Los Angeles families celebrate Thanksgiving in their own ways.

2. A young hippie is busted for littering.

3. An uptight family man and an extraordinarily annoying salesman are repeatedly thrown together while trying to get home for Thanksgiving.

4. Director Jodi Foster turns choreographer when the turkey does a lap dance.

5. "You cut da toikey" A tight knit extended family unravels when one couple arrives late for Thanksgiving dinner.

6. A disaffected 1970's teen explains the true meaning of Thanksgiving to her family.

7. A family obsessed with JFK goes haywire.

8. A family attempt to keep up together after their matriarch dies.

9. A dying mother and an estranged suburban family attempt Thanksgiving together at one daughter's East Village flat.

10. Two country music greats eat their first Thanksgiving together. One of them finally confronts his alcoholic father.

Here are some holiday films for adult sensibilities I can recommend:

Christmas

A Midnight Clear -World War II Soldiers Share a Stille Nacht

A Christmas Carol

Babes in Toyland

Christmas in Connecticut

Dekalogue- A great series by my favorite director, Krzysztoff Kieslowski

Fanny and Alexander-The Christmas everyone will want to have

The Dead

Holiday

The Lion in Winter-neither stockings nor tinsel here, but it takes place on Christmas.

Thanksgiving

What's Cookin'?

Avalon -A view of American family life through the 20th century

Alice's Restaurant

Planes, Trains, and Automobiles

The House of Yes

Fathers' Day and Mothers' Day Meals

A Sunday in the Country

Catfish in Black Bean Sauce

Eat Drink Man Woman

Tortilla Soup

Daddy Nostalgia

Manon of the Spring and Jean de Florette

Catfish in Black Bean Sauce

Joy Luck Club

Great adult Halloween flicks include:

The Haunting-The original only!

Turn of the Screw

The Others

Night of the Hunter-The original only! The only film Charles Laughton ever directed with Robert Mitchum, Shelly Winters, Lillian Gish.

Vicious Victuals and Fatal Food Trivia Quiz

Hollywood revels in the murderous possibilities of kitchens. After all, that's where the knives are. Sometimes screenwriters get a little more creative. Name the unusual implement of dispatch in the following films:

Torn Curtain

A Perfect Murder

Eating Raoul

Attack of the Killer Refrigerator

And you thought all you had to fear from food were calories and cholesterol! Can you name five films where the common concept of a person attacking a plate of food is reversed? Five points each where the food bites back!

Name some films where one way or another food turns out to be fatal.

1. A group of gourmands eat themselves to death.

2. A drama critic is force-fed a minced poodle pie by an irate actor.

3. A young Spanish man is killed by his rival who beats him with a ham

4. An old Mafioso is administered a dose of lye in his coffee.

5. A Yugoslavian sailor dies in a vat of sugar.

6. An opera patron is poisoned by a luscious looking canolli.

Hannibal's Pals and Meat the USDA Didn't Inspect Trivia Quiz

Cannibalism may be one of the enduring taboos of human society, but movies have sold a lot of popcorn tweaking our taboos. If lately, Sir Anthony Hopkins seems to have the franchise on serving his fellow man, he stands in a long, if not particularly noble, dramatic tradition. Cannibalism has been the bill of fare of so many horror films and sharp-toothed satires, the mind reels (and the stomach turns). You'll pardon us if we don't include any of those recipes.

The winner should be awarded a package of gourmet sausages such as Aidells.

1. Anthony Hopkins serves Jessica Lange her sons in the film version of an early Shakespearean drama. Give the full title of this grisly play.

2. Which Golden Age Hollywood actor had his screen swan song in "Soylent Green"?

3. Which character in "The Cook, The Thief, His Wife and Her Lover" ends up as dinner?

4. Aussie heartthrob Guy Pearce squares off against omnivorous Trainspotter Robert Carlisle in which film?

Name at least five films in which meat dishes of suspect origins appear.

5. How does Aunt Lee find all that tasty meat?

6. Who thought you could find such a tasty hamburger in New Zealand?

7. All delis carry exotic looking meats, don't they?

8. Doctors claim new mothers should eat plenty of protein in...

9. "It's the sauce, officer."

10. Don't check in or you may check out as a sausage.

11. Whatever are mom and dad up to in the kitchen?

12. There's a tail behind the making of these yummy pork buns.

Can you name twenty or more other films involving cannibalism? Did you know there were so many?

CHAPTER NINE

Covered With Chocolate (Germany 2001)

Covered with chocolate. Those three words are balm to the soul of any lover of chocolate, whether what is covered is a humble graham cracker or partners in an erotic encounter.

Chocolat

(US 1999)

Lasse Hallstrom directed from the novel by Joanne Harris. With Juliette Binoche, Alfred Molina, Judi Dench, and Johnny Depp (who claims that he doesn't even like chocolate)

Juliette Binoche plays a widowed mother who literally blows into a grim French town then changes the lives of the villagers through the confections she sells at her sweet shop. A pinch of hot Mayan chili tempered by chocolate is what it takes to warm the blood of the unhappy villagers. The filmmakers, trying to make mounds of brown dyed plaster of Paris look like the real thing used Mayan style chocolate molds; real chocolate can't hold up under brilliant set lighting. At least the actors got to taste good chocolate created by a Swiss chocolatier in the many scenes where they enjoy the offerings.

When screening Chocolat there are many options for entertainment. You can serve a light and simple meal followed by a rich chocolate dessert, you can serve just a chocolate dessert and coffee, or you might host a chocolate tasting. The only thing you must not do is to leave viewers with no chocolate at all.

The endless delicacies that food lover and cookbook author Joanne Harris included in her book were too numerous to appear in the film. But I have combined both film and book to create our menu.

My Menu

Arugula Salad in Cumin Vinaigrette
Simple Tomato Soup
French Bread and butter
Chocolate Fondue
Nipples of Venus
Vianne's Hot Chocolate

Simple Tomato Soup

1 lb fresh or two large tins of tomatoes, chopped
1 large yellow onion, chopped
4 T butter or olive oil
2 T sugar
2 cups milk or half and half
Salt and pepper to taste

1. Melt the butter in a medium sized saucepan and sweat the onions until they are soft.
2. Add the tomatoes, the sugar; the salt and pepper then cook over medium heat.
3. When cooked all the way down, about ten to fifteen minutes, remove from heat.
4. Sieve the mixture or force through a food mill to get rid of the skins and seeds, if desired.

5. Add the cream or half and half until your desired consistency is achieved.
6. Heat through gently without boiling and season to taste.

Premade chocolate fondue is available at the grocer's, but it's more fun and perfectly easy to experiment with your own.

Chocolate Fondue

⅓ cup whipping cream
8 oz. semisweet or bittersweet chocolate, chopped, preferably SharffenBerger, Valrhona or Callebaut but you can use any chocolate you like.

To your taste:
1½ t orange zest
3 t any orange liqueur

Or

3 t framboise, kirsch, or crème de cassis

Or
¼ t almond or mint or orange extracts

1. Add the cream and the chocolate and heat gently over low heat until melted.
2. Then add whatever flavoring you decide upon.
3. If you haven't got a fondue pot serve the fondue in the cooking pot placed on a coaster. Be careful not to touch the hot pot!
4. If the chocolate begins to thicken put it back on the flame until it melts again.

Pierce your choice of:
Bits of pound, angel food, or sponge cake
Strawberries

Cherries, fresh, frozen or brandied
Sliced bananas, pears, or kiwis
Candied ginger or coconut
Fresh coconut
Nuts
Dates
Figs
Dried fruits
Almond or coconut macaroons
Cookies
Marshmallows

Arrange your tidbits on pretty serving dishes. You can use bamboo skewers for piercing and dipping the goodies. Or regular forks for that matter.

Chocolate Tasting Party

To stage a chocolate tasting party buy as many different kinds of chocolate as you can.

Local favorites can be pitted against national brands. See how American chocolate compares to European. Try Sees, Ghirardelli, Scharffenberger, Fran's, deBrand, Guittard, Hersheys, Godiva, Teuscher, Lindt, Cadbury, Toblerone, or Maison du Chocolat. This is the perfect time to try out boutique chocolatiers such as Vosges Haut from Chicago, LA Burdick from New Hampshire, Jacques Torres in Brooklyn, or XOX Truffles, Ricchuitti, or Charles in San Francisco. Or take a look at bittersweetcafe.com.

Be certain to provide guests plenty of hot black coffee or glasses of ice-cold milk to wash down all that chocolate.

Nipples of Venus appear in Chocolat and also in Amadeus.

Chocolat author Joanne Harris features a recipe for Nipples of Venus in her cookbook "My French Kitchen." I've adapted it for utmost simplicity. You do not need to temper the chocolate in this recipe. To temper, chocolate is brought to a certain temperature then reduced.

This process makes for a glossier result, but does not improve the taste of the chocolate.

Nipples of Venus

8 oz. high-quality dark chocolate, finely chopped Sharffen Berger, Valrhona or Callebaut are all good, but you can use any chocolate you like
1 ¼ cups heavy whipping cream
4 oz. dark chocolate, finely chopped, for dipping
2 oz. high-quality white chocolate, finely chopped, for the final dip

1. Gently heat the cream.
2. Immediately after it comes to the boil, pour it over chopped chocolate.
3. Allow to cool for at least two hours, and then whip with a hand blender until stiff enough to pipe.
4. Pipe with a #7 tip through a pastry bag onto a parchment lined cookie sheet into a nipple shape.
5. Chill in the refrigerator.
6. Then, in a double boiler (or just a pan of simmering water with a bowl placed over it) melt the dark chocolate.
7. Dip the nipples until covered with warm chocolate.
8. Cool again.
9. Melt the white chocolate then dip the tip of the nipples in and let cool. Voila.

This is based on author Joanne Harris's version of her character's cocoa.

Vianne's Hot Chocolate

1 ⅔ cup milk
½ vanilla bean
½ cinnamon stick
1 hot red chili seeded
3 ½ oz. bittersweet chocolate 70%, grated

1. Add the bean, stick, and chili to the milk in a sturdy saucepan.
2. Simmer gently for one minute.
3. Add the chocolate and remove from heat.
4. Stir.
5. Let infuse to ten minutes.
6. Remove stick, bean, and chili then reheat.
7. Serve.
8. You can add sugar to taste if this is too much for you!

Vatel

(UK-France 2000)

Roland Joffe directed Uma Thurman, Gerard Depardieu, and Julian Sands.

Vatel may be the ultimate chef film, combining the stories of the actual French royal cook Vatel and the ancient Roman Apicius (who actually did kill himself following a culinary disaster) In the summer of 1661 an incredible party was given at the newly built chateau, Vaux le Vicomte, to impress King Louis the XIV.

French haute cuisine reached its zenith during the reign of the Sun King and viewers will witness the toil as well as the creativity that it took to present swans carved from ice, towering vertical fruit arrangements that take four waiters to carry, and intricate spun sugar constructions.

"Chocolate and the King are my only passions," Queen Maria Theresa, wife of Louis XIV is supposed to have claimed. It's a good thing for her that she enjoyed chocolate because the King was not passionate about poor Marie-Therese and she did not attend the fabulous occasion at Vaux le Vicomte.

The characters in Vatel do not perceive hot chocolate as a children's drink or an aid for a good night's sleep. Instead hot cocoa is an alluring accompaniment to seduction. Therefore, the following:

International Hot Chocolates

American

Use Ghirardelli Cocoa. In a pinch serve Nestlé's Quik, as any hot chocolate is better than none. Pour into mugs or cups into which a marshmallow has been dropped.

Dutch

2 T Droste cocoa
2 t sugar
1 cup milk

1. Mix the cocoa and sugar.
2. Add just enough water or milk or cream to make a paste.
3. Add one cup hot milk.

Mexican

For a spicy treat follow the instructions on the package or
4 T unsweetened cocoa powder
4 T sugar
2½ cups whole milk
3 oz. bittersweet chocolate, chopped
½ vanilla bean, split
½ ground cinnamon
¼ t ground nutmeg
¼ t ancho chili powder
Whipped cream-optional

1. Mix powder and sugar.
2. Heat milk in a medium saucepan over low heat.
3. Add the all the ingredients.
4. Whisk while heating without boiling.

Viennese

Add a dollop of whipped cream to prepared cocoa, and then sprinkle with cinnamon.

French

2 cups milk
1 cup water
2 oz dark chocolate
½ ounce cocoa powder, preferably Maison du Chocolat

Add the grated rind of one orange after bringing to a boil.
Or
3 T chocolate powder Maison du Chocolat or Bernachon.
3 t boiling water
Make a paste and leave overnight.
2 cups whole milk
2 T sugar

Boil the milk and sugar.
Add the paste and blend.

To dress up your cocoa you may add instant coffee or espresso; liqueurs such as Kahlua, cognac or Amaretto; vanilla, almond or peppermint extract; cinnamon or nutmeg; or use honey or brown sugar instead of white sugar.

Chocolate Pots de Crème

Although recipes exist that include liqueurs, zests, and various chocolates this one is as simple as pots de crèmes gets. If you use a bitter sweet chocolate this dessert will have a sophisticated adult flavor. Sweeter chocolate will result in a more traditional pudding.

1 cup heavy cream
2 oz. good sweetened chocolate, melted (microwave)
2 egg yolks

Boiling water

1. Preheat oven to 325.
2. Heat the cream gently in a double boiler, bain-marie or carefully in a good saucepan.
3. Add the chocolate and blend.
4. Beat the yolks and then add the hot cream stirring all the while.
5. Pour into ramekins or pots de crèmes pots.
6. Place in a baking pan that is filled with hot water one inch up the pot.
7. Bake for 25 to 30 minutes or until firm.

Cross Creek

(US 1983)

Martin Ritt directed Mary Steenburgen, Peter Coyote, and Malcolm MacDowell

Steenburgen portrays novelist Marjorie Kinnan Rawlings (The Yearling) as she adjusts to rural life in 1920's Florida. Chocolate cake makes a guest appearance twice in this film along with pecan pie, sassafras tea and hooch. Rawlings neighbors host a "pound party" also known as a pounding, a form of potluck where every guest brings a pound of something to eat. But at this "party" Rawlings is the only guest. She enjoyed cooking and in fact wrote a cookbook, "Cross Creek Cookery."

Chocolate Layer Cake

The flavors deepen in this cake after a day or two.

3 ½ cups flour

1 cup granulated sugar

½ cup packed brown sugar

½ cup unsweetened cocoa

2 t powder

1 t soda

½ t salt

3 eggs
½ cup sour cream
6 T unsalted butter
½ cup oil
1 ¼ cups cold water
I T vanilla
Cream cheese
1 ½ cups powered cocoa

1. Preheat the oven to 350.
2. Flour and butter two 8 inch round cake pans.
3. Combine the sugars, the cocoa, and the other dry ingredients.
4. Blend the eggs, cream, and vanilla.
5. Combine the butter, oil, and water.
6. Blend the flour mixture, then the egg mixture with the oil mixture.
7. Beat until smooth.
8. Divide the batter evenly into the pans.
9. Bake for 50 to 55 minutes until a toothpick stuck into the middle of the cakes comes out clean.

Frosting

3 cups of powdered sugar, sifted with
⅔ cup unsweetened powdered cocoa
4 oz. of cream cheese
1 t vanilla
5 or more T milk

1. Add the cream cheese to the cocoa mixture.
2. Blend until smooth adding the vanilla and enough milk to make a spreadable consistency as you go.

What to drink with chocolate beside a tall glass of cold milk? Champagne of course! Sweet wines such as ice wines or Elysium Quady. Sherry such as Pedro Ximenez, or tawny port such as Pedro Ximenez, or, Madeira, are well known for their compatibility with sweets, but there are some reds that complement chocolate well; Heron Cabernet Sauvignon, Fetzer Zinfandel, Arrowood Sonoma County Cabernet Sauvignon. White wines are not usually the best accompaniment to chocolate unless they are very sweet.

Chocoholics Trivia Quiz

Chocolate has long been regarded as an aphrodisiac so in the movies chocolate is frequently synonymous with sensual indulgence. Name several film titles where chocolate is nearly a leading character.

Name:

1. The Mexican flick in which a chef literally cooks up passion.

2. Briton Mike Leigh's film that combines fudge sauce and foreplay.

3. The Charlie-starved adaptation of Roald Dahl's cautionary fable.

4. It could only happen in the movies: a film in which a French community is wholly ignorant of either romance or cocoa.

5. A Balzac adaptation wherein a manipulative maiden lady discovers a risqué chanteuse and her sculptor amant sharing a roll in the chocolat.

6. Two nineteen fifties housewives try out the working life at a chocolate factory

Whoever answered those easy ones correctly gets a packet of Milk Duds. For extra credit and maybe a Godiva truffle come up with the following titles. Apropos gifts for the winner includes Chocolate Therapy Kit, Chocoholic's Kit, Body Talk Tattoo Kit, or Body Frosting.

1. A Canadian lesbian couple experience parent trouble.

2. A "10" spends her billions on a French truffle factory.

3. A French colonial woman (vanilla) and a local man (chocolate) interact in Cameroon.

4. Isabelle Huppert, a chocolate company executive, and her pianist husband befriend a young man.

5. A young woman leaves her Canadian village with a dark secret.

6. In Cuba, a gay man and a straight revolutionary form a complicated friendship.

7. An Italian immigrant to Switzerland tries to make himself more like the Swiss but his attempt is full of holes.

8. A fantasy among the pastries.

9. Dawn French, playing a portly London schoolteacher, juggles the men in her life.

10. A teenage loup garoux has greater worries than if chocolate causes acne.

CHAPTER TEN

Monsoon Wedding (2001)

Get-Togethers for the Wedding Party

In wedding scenes from Goodbye Columbus to Father-of the Bride the unexpected is always to be expected. Too often the in-laws are hopelessly snobbish, the groom is preposterously late, the wedding cake gets smashed, a relative becomes obnoxiously drunk or a well-dressed guest winds up in the swimming pool. We watch again and again as the groom tries a near toxic folk remedy to treat a hangover after his stag party, an ex-spouse or former flame rears a well-coifed head, the ring goes missing, or the bride runs away in full white regalia. Movie wedding scenes are as repetitive as the nuptial vows themselves.

There's rarely a simple little ceremony in a movie. Even people of humble means seem capable of hosting weddings with a greenhouse worth of flowers, large and talented bands, a huge quantity of food and the best champagne. They have vast and healthy lawns, perfectly decorated households, guests who follow the dress code, and enormous tranquil swimming pools awaiting disaster.

Two films, Monsoon Wedding and My Big Fat Greek Wedding caught the imaginations of a huge viewing public perhaps because neither depicts the overblown generic WASP wedding.

Monsoon Wedding

(India 2001)

Directed by Mira Nair with Vijay Raaz, Naseeruddin Shah, and Vasundhara Das.

A new romance blossoms, an old family friendship rots on the vine, and the wedding couple may actually be falling in love, in this charming, exuberant, and intoxicating film.

Every wedding is a Monsoon Wedding to members of the wedding party. They are whirlwinds of activity. Colors not seen on any other day (the bridesmaids dresses and shoes), the scent of more flowers than even at a funeral, the snatched snippets of conversations with old friends and distant family members, the flaring tempers, the opposing wishes, the nerves, the doubts about the wisdom of the marriage itself.

I've devised an easy to prepare Indian meal to go with this wonderful evocation of a universal experience set in an exotic, yet modern, environment. But you can also opt for Indian takeout or visit your grocery store where you will find an array of prepared sauces that you can use for chicken, beef, lamb, or vegetable curry dishes.

Play the soundtrack CD of Monsoon Wedding. Use fragrant flowers and frangipani votives. Find your most exotic looking serving dishes, scatter pillows throughout the living room and serve dinner on the coffee table.

Lentil Dal
Beef Curry
Kashmir Lamb Curry
Coriander and Coconut Chicken
Cauliflower Curry
Basmati rice
Sliced Tomatoes and Cucumbers with Lime
Nan, chapatti or kulcha (if you cannot obtain Indian breads purchase some packaged pita rounds from your grocer)
Coconut and Mango Sorbets
Kingfisher Beer
Assorted wines
Chai

Lentil Dal

1 cup lentils
1 large onion chopped
2 green peppers, chopped
2 T butter
½ t turmeric
1 t salt
1 t dry mustard
1 t coriander

1. Soak lentils for one hour.
2. Drain.
3. Sauté onions and pepper in butter.
4. Add lentils, turmeric and enough water to cover.
5. Boil and then simmer until lentils are tender, checking to see if more water is needed.
6. Add salt, mustard and coriander.
7. Blend.

Serve with a Pinot Blanc, Riesling, red or white Cote du Rhone, a light Pinot Noir, or Dry Rose.

Simple Beef Curry

½ cup peanut oil
2 large onions, chopped
5 to six garlic cloves, sliced
3 T curry paste
3 T tamarind paste
2 pounds chuck steak, cubed
Salt

1. Heat the oil then fry the onions.
2. Then add the garlic and fry, being careful not to burn it.
3. Add the curry mixtures, then the meat.
4. Cover and simmer for two hours until meat is tender.
5. Add salt.

Kashmir Lamb Curry

2 pounds boned shoulder of lamb, cubed
1 cup sour cream
2 t garam masala
4 t curry powder
½ cup butter or ghee (clarified butter)
3 T blanched almonds
¾ cup raisins
¾ cup dried apricots, thinly sliced
4 garlic cloves, sliced
2 inch piece of fresh ginger
2 large onions
Lemon juice

1. Marinate beef in sour cream and spices for several hours. Heat butter in a saucepan.
2. Sauté the almonds until golden.
3. Then sauté the garlic lightly and remove.
4. Fry the onions until golden.
5. Add the meat and marinade.
6. Cook five minutes.
7. Add the fruit.
8. Cover and simmer forty five to sixty minutes.
9. Add salt and lemon juice and garnish with almonds.

Serve with a Syrah, a Pinot Blanc, a Riesling, or a Pinot Grigio,

Chicken with Coriander and Coconut Milk

1 t ginger root, minced
1 small yellow onion, finely chopped
2 T salt
4 cloves garlic, finely chopped

Blend in a blender or Cuisinart then spread over:

3 pounds chicken legs and thighs

Brown the chicken in 6 T oil until brown. Remove the meat from the pan.

8 T oil or ghee if available

Combine:
1 cup plain yogurt
½ cup evaporated milk
8 strands of saffron
1 t salt

Add 2 T oil to the frying pan and fry for one minute
2 T blanched, sliced almonds
2 T raisins

Add the yogurt mixture. Add the chicken and
1 cup fresh coriander finely chopped
1 minced green chili
Cook for about 8 minutes
Add 2 cups coconut milk
Reduce heat and simmer for forty five minutes until chicken is tender.
Serve over rice.

Riesling, Franc Rose, Chenin Blanc, Sauvignon Blanc, Champagne, Viognier, could all go well with this dish.

Cauliflower Curry

1 large cauliflower
¼ cup yogurt
1 onion, grated
2 garlic cloves crushed
1 t sugar
1 t ginger
¼ cup butter
1 t salt
2 cups hot water

½ t ground cinnamon
¼ t nutmeg
¼ t coriander

1. Clean the cauliflower and separate into flowerets.
2. Put the yogurt in a large bowl and ad to onion, garlic, ginger and sugar.
3. Add the cauliflower and marinate for at least two hours.
4. Stir now and again.
5. Heat the butter in a sauté pan.
6. Add the grated onions to it and brown them.
7. Add the cauliflower and its marinade.
8. Add salt and water and cook for twenty minutes until tender. A thick sauce should have formed.
9. Remove and sprinkle with coriander, nutmeg, and cinnamon.

And down it all with hot or iced chai or some Indian beer.

Garam Masala

1 T freshly ground nutmeg
½ t ground cloves
1 t mace
1 t ground cardamom
¼ t cayenne pepper
2 ¼ t ground coriander
½ t caraway
1 ½ t paprika
2 ½ t anchovy paste
2 t vinegar

Combine and keep in an airtight jar.

Curry Paste

½ cup garam masala
½ cup black pepper
6 T caraways
2 ½ T ground cinnamon
½ cup coriander
2 ½ T cloves, ground
2 T cardamom seeds
Plum jam
Lemon juice

1. Remove any husks.
2. Grind in coffee grinder.
3. Add equal parts plum jam and lemon juice until a paste forms.
4. Keep in fridge.

My Big Fat Greek Wedding
(US 2002)

Joel Zwick directed with Nia Vardolos who wrote and starred with John Corbett, Lainie Kazan, and Michael Constantine.

Toula leads a dull life as an over obedient daughter until she blossoms and falls in love with a man outside her ethnicity. Cultural comedy prevails in this enjoyable romp.

Get the soundtrack CD or even Zorba the Greek.

Lettuce, Greek Olives, Feta
Artichokes and Rice
Lamb Chops with Feta
Baklava

Artichokes and Rice

6 small artichokes
1 onion, minced
2 T fresh dill or dry dill
3 T chopped parsley
Olive oil
2 lemons
2 t chicken stock (fresh, canned, or bouillon cube)
1 cup raw rice
Salt and pepper

1. Wash the artichokes.
2. Remove three or four layers of the outer leaves.
3. Slice an inch off the tips.
4. Cut into quarters and remove the furry parts.
5. Place in a bowl of water and add the juice of one lemon.
6. In a casserole sauté the onions, parsley and dill in one half cup of olive oil.
7. Rinse and drain the chokes.
8. Then sauté them with this mixture for five minutes.
9. Add two cups of water and cook for twenty minutes.
10. Add the rice and chicken stock. Stir and simmer for thirty minutes.
11. When the rice is cooked sprinkle the juice of one lemon over the mixture.
12. Heat a couple of T of olive oil and pour over the rice.
13. Cover for five minutes.
14. Serve.

For spur of the moment recreation of this dish you can use drained artichoke hearts from a jar. Sauté the bottled hearts with the onions and parsley and add to prepared rice. Sprinkle with dill, olive oil, lemon juice, salt and pepper.

WINE

If you feel brave you might try the traditional red wine of Corfu, Ropa. Retsina, served very chilly is a more palatable choice, but for easily drinkable wines try a simple crisp white from Friuli in Italy or a light, crisp Alsatian. Roses from Provences or perhaps a simple, fruity, young red would be serviceable.

A relatively high acid dish, this lamb requires a higher acid wine. A clarety Zinfandel like Storybook Mountain or Hidden Cellars would be good. A youngish, well structured Bordeaux would work.

Lamb Chops with Feta

4 lamb chops
2 cloves garlic
4 T olive oil
½ t each of thyme and oregano
Pepper
Salt
4 oz. feta cheese
1 large ripe tomato, chopped

1. Cut a pocket into the chops with a sharp knife or have your butcher do it.
2. Crush the garlic.
3. Combine the garlic with the pepper and rub it into both sides of the meat.
4. Heat the oil in a skillet and sauté the chops on both sides for about three minutes on each side until they are browned. Crumble the herbs and feta together and put into the pocket along with the tomatoes.
5. Broil under a broiler for up to seven minutes until the meat is slightly firm.

Monsoon Weddings Trivia Quiz

1. A hurricane disrupts the big day for Ben Affleck and Sandra Bullock.

2. ABBA is a wannabe bride's raison d'etre.

3. The bride is so drugged up she can barely stand.

4. With best a friend like her, who needs enemies?

5. He sings.

6. In Alabama, a train kills the bride's brother on her wedding day.

7. A Gypsy farce.

8. The bride runs off and hops public transportation with her mother's lover.

9. The bride runs away again and again.

10. Sprinklers on a golf course soak the mother of the bride and the mentally challenged sister.

11. Cajun dancers look like they're having the best time of all the guests in this Magnolia strewn wedding.

12. How many nuptials and an interment?

13. A jittery bride lolls on her bed while her sister, her editor, her Dad, the groom's best friends, her therapist, and finally the groom, try to coax her out to complete the ceremony.

14. There's a last minute change in grooms in this classic film and its remake.

15. A great Jewish wedding scene where, although all the guests are made fun of, they really look like they're having fun.

16. A wannabe songwriter who was left at the altar.

17. You endured their courtship; now witness their marriage in this sequel.

18. The Rape of the Oregonian Women.

19. Gay guys from Taiwan.

20. Tribulations of the parent.

CHAPTER ELEVEN

Snack and Drink (US 1999)

What To Eat and Drink With Your Favorite Films

"The man said it was very good champagne. Should I bring the potato chips?"

— Marilyn Monroe in The Seven Year Itch

You may not want to prepare all the feasts depicted in many films, but that doesn't mean you have to settle for microwave popcorn while viewing a video. The lolly-ices (popsicles) in A Clockwork Orange, the box of chocolates in Forrest Gump, the exotic nipples of Venus in Amadeus, and tiramisu, from Sleepless in Seattle, are only a few of the dozens of luscious beverages and delectable edibles that make cameo appearances in films.

Champagne rears its bubbly head in hundreds of films. Whether you want to join Marilyn Monroe in drinking champers and munching potato chips in The Seven Year Itch, or Rick and Ilse, who consider drinking up all the champagne before the Germans get it in Casablanca, you'll never go wrong popping a cork while watching a film.

8 Women

(France 2002) Francois Ozon directed Isabelle Huppert, Fanny Ardant, and Catherine Deneuve.

As a child, Ozon was struck by the Super 8 images his father had filmed in India of dead hippos floating in the Ganges amid playing children. He says this made him understand "that it didn't take a lot of money or equipment to tell a story, to convey feelings and emotions." The images in 8 Women as are far from dead hippos as you can get since the crème de la crème of French actresses sashay in their fashions, sing, dance, and connive in this delightful cocktail of a film.

I've devised a girls'- night-in party anyone could enjoy. Have your guests wear vintage cocktail attire, preferably each in a different color. Have plenty of ice on hand and use vintage cocktail glasses and cocktail napkins. Play the 8 Women soundtrack CD. Then break out these unusual cocktails. Don't try all of them unless your guests bring their sleeping bags and you have Alka Seltzer on tap. You might ask the guests to guess which of the cocktails you do serve represents which characters once they've seen the film.

Each of these cocktails represents one of the eight women characters in the film.

Homecoming~For all the characters

1 oz amaretto
1 oz Irish cream

Pink Lady for Suzot as portrayed by Virginie Ledoyen

1 ½ oz gin,
1 ½ oz cream
1 t grenadine

Nasty Girl for Catherine as portrayed by Ludivine Sagnier

¾ oz Drambuie
¼ oz amaretto
¼ oz banana liqueur
¼ oz peach schnapps

Nervous Breakdown for Augustine as played by Isabelle Huppert

Despite the name this one sounds like a good bet for modern girls.

1½ oz vodka
½ oz black raspberry liqueur
Cranberry juice
Lime
Soda

Scarlet Letter

This pretty drink is a little lighter than some, so you can drink more!

¾ glass champagne
Black raspberry liqueur
Dash cranberry juice

White Mink for Catherine de Neuve as Gaby

1 oz Galliano
1 oz triple sec
And 1 oz milk
Pour over ice and strain

Merry Widow for Danielle Darrieux as Mama

1 ¼ oz cherry brandy
1 ¼ oz maraschino
Ice and strain.

Black Lady for Firmine Richard as Chanel the Maid

2 oz. orange liqueur
½ oz coffee liqueur
½ oz brandy ice and strain

Bend Me Over for Emmanuelle Beart as Louise the Maid

1 oz vodka
1 oz amoretto
1 oz sour mix
Ice

Cocktail Trivia Quiz

Food isn't the only focus in films. Cocktails are often prominent and some plots revolve around drinking establishments, most often a seedy dive.

Can you think of several drinking films without getting a hint? Double your score for every right answer without a hint. The winner should be given a cocktail accoutrement such as amusing olive spears and the phone number of Alcoholics Anonymous.

1. Jack Lemmon leads wife Lee Remick into a life of drink.

2. Ray Milland invites viewers along on a four-day bender.

3. A straitlaced guy has one too many in this silent feature.

4. A drunken British diplomat self-destructs in 1930's Mexico.

5. Jack Nicholson belatedly fesses up to dropping the baby while he was inebriated.

6. Jackie Chan utilizes an interesting style of Kung Fu.

7. Mickey Rourke and Faye Dunaway tie them on at an LA dive.

8. Barkeep Tom Arnold comments on his customers' woes.

9. Tom Cruise turns from scientology to mixology.

10. Dancing on the bar reaches heights of glory.

11. Five friends reunite at a New Jersey dive.

12. Steve Buscemi concludes he's a born loser while drowning his sorrows at his haunt, a New Jersey tavern.

13. Mel Gibson and restaurant owner Michelle Pfeiffer share misadventures.

14. Misfits wander into a depression era San Francisco dive and leave a little better for it in this adaptation of a William Saroyan play.

15. Its Four Beers and a Funeral when friends get together and drink following the suicide of their friend.

16. Two guys struggle to make a go at running a neighborhood bar.

17. Two men visit California's "other" wine country.

Can you identify these famous snippets of spirited dialogue?

1. "Vodka martini, shaken not stirred."

2. "He's dragged me into every gin mill on the block."

3. "Waiter bring me five more martinis," says a charming woman who is trying to keep up with her husband who has already downed six.

4. "Let's get something to eat. I'm thirsty."

5. ...He'll water his garden with Champagne before he let the Germans drink it.

6. Champagne is the great leveler.

Beverage Suggestions By Movie

Breakfast at Tiffany's Champagne and orange juice mimosas

Like Water for Chocolate-Mexican hot chocolate

Moulin Rouge-see below

Soylent Green -Green Kool-Aid

The Fanny Trilogy -French aperitifs

The God's Must Be Crazy -Coca Cola

The Seven Year Itch -Champagne and Potato Chips

The Thin Man Series -Martinis or Sidecars-See below

The Time of Our Lives -Pincon Punch

And it would always be appropriate to drink one of Francis Ford Coppola's wines from Rubicon Estate. There are cabernets, syrahs, merlots, cabernet francs, zinfandels, a blanconcaux, and a blancs de blancs or a rose sparkling wine named after that other film director Sofia Coppola.

Sidecars

½ jigger of Cointreau
½ jigger of lemon juice
1 ½ jiggers of brandy
¾ cup ice

1. Chill glasses
2. Add ice to glasses
3. Mix drinks
4. Pour over ice and garnish with a twist of lemon

Moulin Rouge

1½ oz. sloe gin
½ ounce sweet vermouth
3 dashes bitters

1. Fill glass with ice.
2. Shake.
3. Strain.

Alternate Moulin Rouge

This is also known as the Bolly-Stoli for Bollinger Champagne and Stolichnaya vodka from the English television show Absolutely Fabulous.

1 ounce vodka
4 oz. champagne

James Bond Martini

3 oz. gin
1 ounce vodka
½ ounce blond Lillet

1. Shake, don't stir.
2. Strain.
3. Garnish with lemon.

A Pizza Trivia Quiz

Cinematically pizza is an opportunity for slapstick and a metaphor for the multi-ethnic mosaic of America. It's also one of America's favorite foods and the most frequent accompaniment to videos shown at home.

1. What film launched the career of Julia Roberts?

2. What Spike Lee morality play centered on a pizza parlor?

3. Which movie is about the tribulations of two friends who work at a pizza parlor?

4. What film is about a pizza delivery guy who will do anything to get the $15.23 owed to him?

5. Which film shows a young man trying to win the love of his high school sweetheart?

SNACK AND DRINK SUGGESTIONS BY MOVIE

A Clockwork Orange -Popsicles
American Beauty -Asparagus Tips
Annie Hall -Anything with lobster
Aunt Lee's Meat Pies -Meat Pies
Cannery Row -Sardines
Cool Hand Luke -Hardboiled eggs with a cellar of salt
Fatso-Carrot sticks
Five Easy Pieces-Sandwiches
Kramer vs. Kramer-French Toast
La Grande Bouffe-Anything
Motel Hell-Sausages
Pie Eating 10-Pie
Polar Express-Hot Cocoa
Popeye-Spinach Spanikopeta
Repo Man-Shrimps and beer
The Road to Wellville-Breakfast Cereal
Shrimp on the Barbie-Shrimp
The Group-Marzipan Candies
Tommy-Baked Beans
White Christmas-Sandwiches and Buttermilk

Pasta

The Apartment
Diary of a Mad Housewife
Spaghetti Westerns
The Linguini Incident
Lady and the Tramp
Chocolate
Bread and Chocolate
Chocolate Inspector
Chocolate Soldier
Covered With Chocolate
Forrest Gump
Life is Sweet
Willie Wonka and the Chocolate Factory
Charlie and the Chocolate Factory

Pastries

Amadeus-Viennese pastries, Nipples of Venus, Viennese coffee
American Pie One and Two-Pie
Animal Crackers
Anna Karenina-Russian Tea Cakes with Russian Caravan tea
Babette's Feast-Tinned Danish cookies and coffee
Cornbread, Earl and Me-Cornbread
Gosford Park-Packaged English biscuits and tea
Rosemary's Baby-Devils Food Cake
Sleepless in Seattle-Tiramisu
The Hours-Chocolate Cake
The Importance of Being Ernest-Packaged English biscuits and tea
The Prime of Miss Jean Brodie- Packaged Scottish shortbread
Twin Peaks- Cherry pie and coffee

Takeout

A Passage to India-Indian Takeout
Career Girl-Fish and Chips
Catfish in Black Bean Sauce-Vietnamese takeout
Delicatessen-French charcuterie
Dim Sum-Dim Sum
Diner-Roast Beef Sandwiches
Mambo kings-Cuban Sandwiches
Monsoon Wedding-Indian Takeout
Mostly Martha-Italian antipasti
Pulp Fiction-Burgers and shakes
The Butcher's Wife-French charcuterie
The Joy Luck Club-Chinese takeout
The Last Emperor-Dim Sum
When Harry Met Sally-Chinese takeout
White Palace-Hamburgers
With Six You Get Egg Roll-Chinese takeout

Fruit

K Pax-Bananas
Oranges Are Not the Only Fruit
Our Vines Have Tender Grapes
The Godfather Series-Oranges
Wild Strawberries

ANSWER KEY

Answers to ENCHANTING EDIBLES from Chapter 1/Dinner with Friends

1) Alice in Wonderland-5 points
2) Chocolat -5
3) Like Water for Chocolate-5
4) Woman on Top-15
5) Snow White and the Seven Dwarf –5
6) Popeye-5

Answers to PLOTS THAT AREN'T SO MEATY from Chapter 1/Dinner with Friends

1) Breakfast Club -5
2) Naked Lunch- 10
3) Guess Who's Coming to Dinner-15
4) The Man Who Came to Dinner -15
5) Breakfast at Tiffany's-5

Some possible answers to FILMS THAT PURPORT TO BE ABOUT MEALS from Chapter 1/Dinner with Friends

A Disturbance at Dinner -15
Bed and Breakfast -15
Breakfast of Champions -10
Chocolate for Breakfast -15
Diamonds for Breakfast -15
Dinner and a Movie -10
Dinner and Driving -15
Dinner at Eight -10
Dinner at Fred's -15
Dinner at the Ritz -15
Dinner for Schmucks -10
Dinner in Purgatory -15
I Want Someone to Eat Cheese With -5
Last Supper -15
Late For Dinner -15
Lobster for Breakfast -15
My Dinner with Oswald -15
Picnic -15
Ploughman's Lunch -15
Price of Sugar -15
Sunday Dinner for a Soldier -20
Tea With Mussolini -10
The Dining Room -10
The Dinner Game -10
The Last Supper -10
The Thief Who came to Dinner -15

Possible answers to FRUITY FILM TITLES from Chapter 1/Dinner with Friends

A Clockwork Orange -5
Bananas -5
Belly Fruit -20

Blood Oranges -15
Coconuts -5
Color of Pomegranate -15
Grapes of Wrath -10
Greengage Summer -20
Our Vines Have Tender Grapes -15
Oranges Are Not the Only Fruit -15
Soft Fruit -15
Sour Grapes -15
Strawberry Fields -15
Taste of Cherry -10
The Scent of Green Papaya -10
The Snapper -15
Three Bites of the Apple -15
What's Eating Gilbert Grape? -10
Wild Strawberries -5

Some possible answers to film titles with plots that have little to do with the food their names celebrate from Chapter 1/Dinner with Friends

American Pie One and Two -10
Animal Crackers -10
Bitter Sugar -15
Bread and Chocolate -10
Bread and Roses -15
Bread and Tulips -10
Brown Sugar -5
Cakes and Ale -15
Candy -20
Canadian Bacon -15
Chicken Run -10
Chocolate Soldier -15
Chop Suey -20
Chutney Popcorn (15
Cider House Rules -15

Cookie -15
Cornbread, Earl and Me -15
Crackerjack -20
Dim Sum -15
Duck Soup -10
Fast Food -10
Food of Love -15
Fortune's Cookie -15
Fortune Cookies -15
Ginger Snaps -15
Green Goddess -20
Ground-hog Day -20
Hamburger Hill -20
Hard Boiled -20
Home Fries -15
Hot Dog-The Movie -15
Hot Pepper -15
Layer Cake -5
Macaroni -15
Meatballs -10
Milk Money -10
Mixed Nuts -15
Picnic -20
Popcorn -15
Pork Chop Hill -15
Salt and Pepper -15
Soup to Nuts -20
Southern Comfort -20
Spaghetti Westerns -25
Sugar and Spice -15
The Apple Dumpling Gang -15
The Corn Is Green -15
The Dish -15
The Gingerbread Man -15
The Honey Pot -15
The Linguini Incident -15
The Magic Pudding -20

The Toast of New Orleans -20
The Toast of New York -20
Turkish Delight -15
Uncle Meat -15
Vanilla Sky -15
Woman Soup -20

Possible answers to SCENES OF UNPARALLELED GLUTTONY from Chapter 2/ The Man Who Came to Dinner

Tommy -15
Magical Mystery Tour -15
Monty Python's The Meaning of Life -20
Cool Hand Luke -10
The Magic Christian -20
La Grande Bouffe -10

Answers for GROSS GRUB and VILE VIANDS *from Chapter 3/A Family Affair*

1. Barefoot in the Park- 20 points
2. Cannery Row-20
3. Career Girls-20
4. The God of Cookery-20
5. The Governess- 15
6. Harold and Maude-15
7. Household Saints-15
8. K-Pax- 5
9. Life is Sweet-10
10. Love in a Cold Climate-15
11. Oliver -5
12. Road Warrior-5
13. Rocky-5
14. Rosemary's Baby- 5

15. Soylent Green -10
16. The Freshman- 10
17. The Van-10
18. Time Regained- Strawberries in Ether 15 points each
19. Bandits-15
20. Elf-10

Answers for QUALITY TIME IT'S NOT from Chapter 3/A Family Affair

1. American Beauty-10
2. Annie Hall-15
3. Bandits
4. Buffalo 66-10
5. Catfish in Black Bean Sauce-10
6. Celebration-20
7. Goodfellas-5
8. Home for the Holidays-5
9. Household Saints-5
10. Myth of Fingerprints-10
11. Secrets and Lies-15
12. The Ice Storm-15
13. Avalon-10
14. The Ref-15
15. Together-15
16. The Birdcage-15
17. Saturday Night Fever-15
18. Meet the Parents-10
19. Mr. Mom

Answers to FOOD ON TELEVISION from Chapter 3/A Family Affair

1) Brideshead Revisted-20
2) Chef-15
3) Duchess of Duke Street-20
4) Hercule Poirot-15
5) The Sopranos-10
6) Twin Peaks-15
7) Upstairs, Downstairs –15
8) I Love Lucy-5
9) I Love Lucy-5
10) Pie in the Sky- 20

Food That Isn't Food Trivia Quiz

1) Laurel and Hardy-10
2) Pink Flamingo-5
3) Salo-15
4) The Gold Rush-10
5) The Three Stooges-10
6) Werner Herzog Eats His Shoe-A documentary by Les Blank-15

Answers for GANGSTER GRUB from Chapter 3/A Family Affair

1) Dinner Rush-5
2) Goodfellas-5
3) Goodfellas-5
4) The Pope of Greenwich Village-15
5) Pope of Greenwich Village-15
6) The Godfather-5
7) The Thief, The Cook, His wife and Her Lover-20

Possible answers to NIBBLING FROM NOVELS from Chapter 4

Five points each

A Christmas Carol-Charles Dickens
Anna Karenina-Leo Tolstoy
Babette's Feast-based on The Feast at Ellsinore by Isak Dinesen
Cannery Row-John Steinbeck
Willie Wonka and the Chocolate Factory based on Charlie and the Chocolate Factory-Roald Dahl
Chocolat-Joanne Harris
Cool Hand Luke-Donn Pearce
Fried Green Tomatoes-Fannie Flagg
The Dead-James Joyce
The Godfather-Mario Puzo
G*one With the Wind*-Margaret Mitchell
Heartburn-Nora Ephron
How Green Was My Valley-Richard Llewellyn
James and the Giant Peach-Roald Dahl
Jean de Florette-Marcel Pagnol
Like Water for Chocolate-Laura Esquival
Little Women-Louisa May Alcott
Passion's Way based on *The Reef*-Edith Wharton
Satyricon-Petronius
The Grapes of Wrath-John Steinbeck
The Group-Mary McCarthy
The Joy Luck Club-Amy Tan
The Leopard-Giuseppe di Lampedusa
The Lion, the Witch, and the Wardrobe-C.S. Lewis
The Little Match Girl-Hans Christian Andersen
The Prime of Miss Jean Brody-Muriel Spark
The Little Princess-Frances Burnett
The Mambo Kings- Oscar Hijuelos
Tom Jones-Henry Fielding
To the Lighthouse-Virginia Wolfe
Women in Love-D.H. Lawrence

Answers to RESTAURANT FILMS from Chapter 5/Dinner Rush

A Chef in Love- 5
Alice's Restaurant-5
Babette's Feast-5
Chef -10
Christmas in Connecticut-5
Consuming Passions-15
Eat Your Heart Out-15
Eating Out-20
Gourmet Zombie Chef from Hell-20
Hamburger College-20
Heavy-20
Pressure Cooker-10
Spanglish-10
Ratatouille-10
Woman on Top-10
Alice Doesn't Live Here Anymore-5
Aunt Lee's Meat Pies-20
Baghdad Café-15
Because I Said So-15
Bed and Breakfast-20
Big Night-5
Blood Diner-20
Christmas in Connecticut-5
Diner-5
Dinner Rush-5
Do the Right Thing-5
Fast Food-15
Fortune Cookie-15
Heartburn-5
In the Weeds-20
Mambo Café-20
Mildred Pierce-15
Mostly Martha-5
Mystic Pizza-5

No Reservations-5
Nude Restaurant-20
Pizza-20
Restaurant-15
Sabrina-5
Shrimp on the Barbi15
Small Time Crooks-5
Spanglish-10
Spitfire Grill-15
That's the Ticket-20
The Butcher's Wife-20
The Cook, the Thief, the Wife and His Lover-5
The Cook-15
The Deli-15
The Harvey Girls20
The Linguini Incident-20
The Pope of Greenwich Village-5
The Van-15
Tortilla Heaven-20
Tortilla Soup-5
Vatel-5
Upstairs, Downstairs-15
White Palace-20
Who's Killing the Great Chefs of Europe? -15
Waitress-15
Woman on Top-15

Chinese Restaurant Films ~20 points each

Of Cooks and Kung Fu
Chicken and Duck Talk
Chicken Rice War
Chinese Feast
Chocolate Inspector
Chungking Express

Cold Dog Soup
Combination Platter
Dragon Inn
Drunken Master
Eat a Bowl of Tea
Eat Drink Man Women
Eating Out
Ermo
House of Luk
Meals on Wheels
Spicy Love Soup
The God of Cookery

French Restaurant Films~20 points each

Aile ou La Cuisse
Après Vous
Au Petit Marguery
Delicatessen
La Cuisine au Beurre
La Grand Restaurant
The Baker's Wife
The Fanny Trilogy

Answers to Movie Stars who Own Restaurants from Chapter 5/Dinner Rush

1. Bill Murray and His Brother own Caddyshack in St. Augustine Florida-20
2. Robert de Niro is part owner of Tribeca in NYC and Rubicon in San Francisco-10
3. Newman's Own is run by Paul Newman's daughter-10
4. Francis Ford Coppola owns Neimann-Copola in San Francisco and Sonoma-10
5. Don Johnson owns Ana Mandara in San Francisco's Ghirardelli Square-20

6. Arnold Schwarzenegger and Demi Moore, Bruce Willis etc., own Planet Hollywood. -10
7. Morgan Freeman owns Ground Zero a blues club specializing in chili burgers at Clarkesdale, Mississippi-20

Answers for Not So Famous Movie Quotes from Chapter 6/Tea and Sympathy

1) Woody Allen-10 points
2) Alfred Hitchcock-15
3) Woody Allen-15
4) Billie Burke-20
5) Groucho Marx-10
6) Barbara Streisand- 20
7) Carol Matthau-20 (Wife of William Saroyan and Walter Matthau)
8) Carmen from Tortilla Soup-20

Answers for Fabulous Food Scenes from Chapter 6/Tea and Sympathy

1) Frenzy-10
2) Duel in the Sun-10
3) The Mysterious Island of Doctor Moreau-15
4) The Apartment-15
5) The Cow and the Prisoner-20
6) Witches of Eastwick-10
7) Mrs. Doubtfire-10
8) Notting Hill-10
9) Giant-10
10) Last Tango in Paris-5
11) The Big Long Trailer-15
12) The Rocky Horror Picture Show-5
13) Annie Hall-5
14) 9 ½ weeks-10
15) The Lady and the Tramp-10

16) Goodbye Columbus-15
17) You Have Mail-10
18) Christmas Story-10
19) Alice in Wonderland-5
20) Chocolat-5
21) Like Water for Chocolate-5
22) Woman on Top-15
23) Snow White-5
24) Gone with the Wind-5
25) Women in Love-10
26) Tampopo-10
27) Realm of the Senses-15
28) A Funny Thing Happened on the Way to the Forum-15
29) What's Up Tiger Lily-10
30) Woman of the Century-15
31) Bridget Jones-15
32) Breakfast at Tiffany's-10

Possible answers for Fighting with Food from Chapter 7/ The Children's Hour

1. Fried Green Tomatoes-5
2. Jamon, Jamon-10
3. Laurel and Hardy-5
4. Any Three Stooges-5 each
5. Hanging On-10

Also:

Animal House -5
Any film with a custard pie -10
Food Fight 1984,1998,2003, 2005 (5 each)
Meatballs -15
Jackass -10

Answers for Turkey Day Trivia Quiz Chapter 8/Home for the Holidays

1. What's Cookin'-15
2. Alice's Restaurant-5
3. Planes, Trains, and Automobiles-5
4. Home for the Holidays-5
5. Avalon-5
6. The Ice Storm-10
7. The House of Yes-10
8. Soul Food -5
9. The Myth of Fingerprints-15
10. Walk the Line-10

Vicious Victuals and Fatal Food Chapter 8/Home for the Holidays

1. Torn Curtain -A gas oven
2. A Perfect Murder -A meat thermometer
3. Eating Raoul -A skillet
4. Attack of the Killer Refrigerator -A give-away the refrigerator

Chapter 8/Home for the Holidays

1. Attack of the Killer Tomatoes-5
2. Attack of the Crab Monster-20
3. Attack of the Giant Mousaka-20
4. Attack of the Killer Hog-20

Chapter 8/Home for the Holidays

1. La Grande Bouffe-5
2. Theatre of Blood -20
3. Jamon, Jamon-15
4. The Pope of Greenwich Village-15

5. Sweet Movie -20
6. Godfather Three -5

Hannibal's Pals Trivia Quiz/Chapter 8/Home for the Holidays

1. Titus Andronicus-10 points
2. Edward G. Robinson-20
3. The Lover-10
4. Ravenous-15
5. Aunt Lee's Meat Pie-15
6. Bad Taste-15
7. Delicatessen-10
8. Flesh Eating Mothers-20
9. Fried Green Tomatoes-5
10. Motel Hell-10
11. Parents-15
12. The Untold Story of Human Meat Roast Pork Buns-20

Some possible answers for other films involving cannibalism:

301, 302-15
Blood Diner-20
Blood -20
Breakfast of Aliens-20
Consuming Passions-20
Crazy Fat Ethyl-20
Demon Barber of Fleet Street-20
Dinner Party-20
Eat and Run-20
Eat the Rich-20
Eat Your Head Off-20
Eating Raoul -10
Gourmet Zombie Chef from Hell -20
How Tasty Was My Little Frenchman-15

I Drink Your Blood-20
I Eat Your Skin-20
Ice Cream Man-20
Keep the River to Your Right-15
Silence of the Lambs-5
Simply Irresistible -20
Theatre of Blood-10
Who is Killing Us? -20

Answers for Chocoholics Trivia Quiz/ Chapter 9/Covered in Chocolate

1. Like Water for Chocolate-5
2. Life Is Sweet-5
3. Willy Wonka and the Chocolate Factory-5
4. Chocolat, 2001-5
5. Cousin Bette-15
6. I Love Lucy-5
7. Better than Chocolate-20
8. Hot Chocolate-15
9. Chocolat, 1995-20
10. Merci pour le Chocolat-10
11. Éclair au Chocolat-20
12. Strawberries and Chocolate-20
13. Bread and Chocolate-20
14. Pain au Chocolat-20
15. Sex and Chocolate-20
16. Blood and Chocolate-10

Answers for Monsoon Weddings/ Chapter 10
5 points each.

1. Forces of Nature
2. Muriel's Wedding
3. Sixteen Candles
4. My Best Friend's Wedding
5. Wedding Singer
6. Fried Green Tomatoes
7. White Cat, Black Cat
8. The Graduate
9. Runaway Bride
10. The Other Sister
11. Steel Magnolias
12. Four Weddings and a Funeral
13. Heartburn
14. Philadelphia Story and High Society
15. Goodbye Columbus
16. Wedding Planner
17. American Wedding
18. Seven Brides for Seven Brothers
19. Wedding Banquet
20. Father of the Bride

Other marriage minded movies:

Honeymoon in Vegas
Arthur
Terms of Endearment
It Had to Be You
Just Married
Bride Wars
Rachel Getting Married
Margot at the Wedding
The Proposal
Bridesmaids
How to Marry a Millionaire: 1 and 2

Answers for Snack and Drinks/Chapter 11

1) Days of Wine and Roses-5 points
2) Lost Weekend-5
3) The Sins of Harold Diddlebock-20
4) Under the Volcano-15
5) Ironweed-10
6) The Drunken Master series-10
7) Barfly -5
8) Barhopping-10
9) Cocktail -5
10) Coyote Ugly-10
11) Last Call-10
12) Tree's Lounge-15
13) Tequila Sunrise-10
14) The Time of Our Lives-20
15) Drinking-20
16) The Tavern-20
17) Sideways-5

Answers for Spirited Dialogue from Chapter 11/Snack and Drink

1) The James Bond Series-5
2) Nora Charles talking about her pooch Asta in *The Thin Man-5*
3) Nora Charles trying to keep up with her husband Nick in *The Thin Man-10*
4) Nick Charles talking to his wife Nora in *After the Thin Man-10*
5) Rick to Ilsa in *Casablanca- 10*
6) Macauly Connor in *The Philadelphia Story*-15

Answers for Pizza Trivia:

1) Mystic Pizza-5
2) Do the Right Thing-5
3) Pizza Runners-15
4) Pizza Man-15
5) Pizza- The Movie-15

RECIPES BY CATEGORY

Appetizers or Snacks

Antipasti

Blinis with Caviar and Crème Fraiche
Taiwanese Marinated Vegetables
Celery with Horseradish Cream Cheese
Cucumber Sandwiches
Escargots Provençal
Figs in Anchovy Vinaigrette
Spicy Grilled Chicken and Grape Skewers
Grilled Vegetable Skewers
Marinated Mushrooms Russian Style
Mushroom Pate
Radishes with Goat Cheese and Chives
Watercress Sandwiches
Welsh Rarebit Savouries
Yogurt Curry Dip

Soups

Ale and Bread Soup
Creamy Vietnamese Soup
Hippy Bean Soup
Italian Garbanzo Soup
Lentil Dal
Pastini in Broth
Potato, Leek, and Ham Soup

Russian Green Cabbage Soup
Tomato Basil Soup
Soupe au Pistou

Salads

Arugula Salad
Avocado in Cumin Lime Vinaigrette
Belgian Endive in Champagne Vinaigrette
Celery, Apple, and Hazelnut Salad
Cucumber, Tomato, and Lime Salad
Curried Noodle Salad
English Summer Salad
Gingerale Jell-O Salad
Monterey Crab and Avocado Salad
Romaine and Curly Endive with Bleu Cheese Dressing
Tomato, Basil, and Mozzarella Salad
Tossed Green Salad with Tarragon or Mustard Vinaigrette

Poultry

Chicken Breasts with White Wine, Cream, and Capers
Chicken Maryland
Honey Grilled Squab
Fresh Coriander and Coconut Chicken
Italian Roast Chicken with Sage and Marsala
Lemon Roasted Game Hen
Babette's Quail with Pate, Truffles, Puff Pastry and Port
Turkey with Fruit, Parmesan and Nut Stuffing

Fish

Chinese Shellfish Salad
Catfish Stew
Tuna in Red Wine Sauce
Fish in Pomegranate Sauce
Lobster Pasta with Champagne Cream Sauce
Martha's Salmon with Basil Sauce

Meat

Bouef en Daube
Irish Spiced Beef Stew
Kashmir Beef Curry
Greek Lamb Chops with Feta and Tomatoes
Lamb Curry
Pork Chops in Mustard Cream Sauce
Rare Roman Rib-eye Steak
Rosemary Roasted Lamb
Cuban Three Citrus Roast Pork

Main Dishes

Dancing Butterfly Cheese Soufflé
Moonstruck Manicotti
Timbale
Big Night Timpano

Vegetables

Braised Peas and Lettuce
Broccolini with Garlic
Carrots à la Parisienne
Cooked Cole Slaw
Cauliflower Curry
Grilled Portobellos
Peas and Prosciutto
Collards with Rice

Side Dishes

Orange Baked Yams
Cuban Black Beans and Rice
Fried Plantains
Potatoes Gratin
Greek Rice with Artichokes and Lemon

Lobster and Pasta in Champagne Cream Sauce
Mac and Cheese
Summer Squash or Pumpkin Risotto
Rice with Peas
Seafood Risotto
Risotto Tricolore
Roman Pasta

Desserts

Almond Blancmange with Berry Jam
Apple and Peach Cobbler
Apple Pudding
Baked Alaska
Cheesecake
Chocolate Fondue
Chocolate Pots de crèmes
Chocolate Sorbet
Cinnamon Flan
Orange Rice Pudding
Floating Island
Gingered Melons
Monte Bianco
Peach Ice Cream
Peach Melba
Plum Pudding
Rhubarb Pudding
Sabrina's Chocolate Mousse
Syllabub
Zuppa Inglese

Cookies, Breads, Cakes & Pies

Almond Polenta Cake
Victoria Sandwich
Cross Creek Chocolate Layer Cake
Daiquiri Bundt Cake

Jewish Honey Cake
Chocolate Peanut Butter Pie
Harvest Fruit Pie
Cornbread
Earth Mother Oatmeal Bread
New England Squash Biscuits
Lemon Cinnamon Muffins
Marijuana Brownies
Palmiers
Pitcaithly Bannock Shortbread
Scones

Candy

Chocolate Leaves
Nipples of Venus
Turkish Delight

Cocktails

Bend Me Over
Bitch Fight
Black Lady
Black Sheep
Corpse Reviver
Dark Secret
Homecoming
Merry Widow
Nasty Girl
Nervous Breakdown
Sidecars
White Mink
Winter Frost
Tiziano
Bellini
Cuba Libres
James Bond Martinis

Tea and Champagne Cocktail
Daiquiris
Moulin Rouges
Bolly- Stoli

Non-Alcoholic Beverages

International Hot Chocolates
Mango Coolers
Vianne's Spicy Cocoa

ABOUT THE AUTHOR

While attending UC Berkeley, Holly Erickson lived next door to the Pacific Film Archive, which she treated as her living room. She graduated from the California Culinary Academy after which she taught cooking, worked at restaurants and catering companies, wrote food articles and restaurants reviews, and worked as a personal chef. She now lives in San Francisco with her daughter and cats, and runs Mrs. Dalloways Catering, which specializes in literary, historical, art, and film themed events.

Capacity

1 t = 5 ml
1 T = 15 ml
1 cup = 240 ml
2 cups (1 pint) = 470 ml
4 cups (1 quart) = .95 liter
4 quarts (1 gal.) = 3.8 liters

Weight

1 fluid oz. = 30 milliters
1 fluid oz. = 28 grams
1 pound = 454 grams

Capacity

5 ml = 1 t
15 ml = 1 T
34 ml = 1 fluid oz.
100 ml = 3.4 fluid oz.
240 ml = 1 cup
1 liter = 34 fluid oz.
1 liter = 4.2 cups
1 liter = 2.1 pints
1 liter = 1.06 quarts
1 liter = .26 gallon

Weight

1 gram = .035 ounce
100 grams = 3.5 oz.
500 grams = 1.10 pounds
1 kilogram = 2.205 pounds
1 kilogram = 35 oz.